CRACKER JACKS
FOR MISFITS

T0149157

CRACKER JACKS
FOR MISFITS

Christine Ottoni

Publishers of Singular
Fiction, Poetry, Nonfiction, Translation, Drama and Graphic Books

Library and Archives Canada Cataloguing in Publication

Title: Cracker Jacks for misfits / Christine Ottoni.
Names: Ottoni, Christine, 1990- author.
Description: Short stories.
Identifiers: Canadiana (print) 20190131462 | Canadiana (ebook) 20190131489 |
    ISBN 9781550968323 (softcover) | ISBN 9781550968330 (EPUB) |
    ISBN 9781550968347 (Kindle) | ISBN 9781550968354 (PDF)
Classification: LCC PS8629.T88 C73 2019 | DDC C813/.6—dc23

Copyright © Christine Ottoni, 2019
Cover art by Adam Winnik
Book designed by Michael Callaghan
Typeset in Garamond, Plantagenet Cherokee, Calibri, and Gill Sans fonts
Published by Exile Editions Ltd ~ www.ExileEditions.com
144483 Southgate Road 14 – GD, Holstein, Ontario, N0G 2A0
Printed and Bound in Canada by Marquis

We gratefully acknowledge the Canada Council for the Arts,
the Government of Canada, the Ontario Arts Council,
and the Ontario Media Development Corporation for their
support toward our publishing activities.

Canadian sales representation:
The Canadian Manda Group,
664 Annette Street,
Toronto ON M6S 2C8 www.mandagroup.com 416 516 0911

North American and international distribution, and U.S. sales:
Independent Publishers Group,
814 North Franklin Street,
Chicago IL 60610 www.ipgbook.com toll free: 1 800 888 4741

For Theresa

JOANNE

UNDER THE HEDGES

I didn't grow up with the devil, but my mother did. I think it's part of what made her get sick. I never met her parents, Arthur and Diana. They came from old-world, farming stock, rural Anglos whose families saved and saved and sent them to the right schools in Montreal so that they would have a shot at a professional life. Arthur loved the track and his Cuban cigars and after he finished McGill, he made a living managing a bank. He met Diana when she was 17 and in her last year boarding at Sacred Heart. They got married and had four girls.

I think Arthur found women, more often than not, to be a complication best understood the way his church told him to: as wives and mothers. He ruled his house strictly. His daughters went to all-girls' school at the Villa, lined up for the Eucharist every Wednesday and Sunday and kept after-school jobs babysitting for Catholic women in the neighbourhood.

That went smoothly when the girls were young but as they grew, certain headstrong, precocious temperaments began to emerge to upset the balance of the household. Martha was the oldest, then my mother, Joanne, then Alexandra and Gillian, just 10 months apart and in the same year at school. Martha was bold and quick, never thinking before she spoke, always dodging a slap. Alex and Gill were a pair, aiding and abetting one another in their frequent truancies from school and church. But my mother was gentle, a little pearl in the boisterous group. She often hid from all the noise in tight, tucked away spaces, behind the dryer in the basement or curled up under the hedges in the backyard.

Joanne had this deep, engrained obedience in her. My dad said she was Arthur's favourite at the expense of Diana's affection. This always felt strange to me, being an only child, that parents should have clear favourites or become jealous of their children. But I never met my grandparents. Maybe they were uncomplicated, envious people. Maybe for them, a father's love was always a threat to a mother's status. Whatever it was, I think Diana knew she got married too young, probably to too religious a man and her frustrations seemed to come out in ways other than her rejection of my mother. She spent her mornings in the bath, soaking in a cloud of steam with her hair up, and her afternoons at the salon. She was a great beauty. A great acquisition when Arthur first met her, and a great source of irritation to him later.

You can see how a man like Arthur would have to do everything in his power to try to keep women like these under control. He cared very much what people thought of him. A country boy with a suit and a car and a tidy white house in Côte Saint-Luc with a yellow door. So he made fire and brimstone rain down in their house, and he put the fear of the devil into his daughters.

The best way I can explain that fear is this. When I was a kid, my mother was unwell a lot. She'd get stuck upstairs in pyjamas and say strange things like she had a voice following her, and it wouldn't leave her alone and my dad would stay home with her, not really knowing what to do. I would kind of sit back and watch the whole thing play out and worry about what would happen to us.

This was before she got on antipsychotics, which allowed her to function pretty well, as long as she took them. Eventually, we found out she had psychosis, real insanity, and her mind would narrow and bend, rearranging the obvious realities of the world. At first her delusions would be harmonious, bright and full of synchronicity, everything in order from raindrops to an orange peel. Everything she saw and touched would manically radiate positive energy and goodwill. But then when things turned bad, as they inevitably would, she was terrified of the devil, of punishment coming for all the bad things she'd done.

I'd ask her, when she was in the middle of various psychic downswings, what exactly she thought she'd done bad. My mother was fundamentally a very good person. Maybe people say that about their mothers, but for mine it was true. She gave money to charity when I was little, and we were house poor. She was shy but did her very best to be friendly to people she passed in the world. She didn't steal or cheat at anything and it was nearly impossible for her to tell a lie, almost to a fault. She loved my father until she couldn't anymore. Even after they separated, she still loved him a lot. But in those moments, when she'd get lock-legged, and peek out of back windows to look up at the sky, teeth chattering, her hands clenched in fists, she'd say her retribution was coming, that God was coming for her, really coming for her this time.

Logic doesn't hold ground in moments like these, so it was better to listen and encourage her back onto her medication, if possible. But the things she was afraid of being paid back for had a quantifiably religious tone, like how she'd had sex before marriage and had gotten separated from my father. She'd never had me baptized or spread the word of Christ in me. She'd forsaken her father and mother. She gave in to lust.

My mother was certain that she had proof of sin and she told me a story once, only once, of how she came to this certainty. It was the summer, the late Seventies, I think, and she was 15 and her sisters had all started smoking. They'd steal their mother's cigarettes from her bedside table and lock themselves up in their bedroom. That summer was the first they were all teenagers and they spent a lot of time in their room, playing records, ironing their hair, and smoking out their window.

That window looked over the front porch roof and it was easy to sneak in and out. They weren't allowed to date but they did anyway. Boys came for them in the night, parking up the street away from Arthur's watchful eye. The girls would crawl back in through their bedroom window as the sun came up, smelling like sweat and peppermint schnapps and Benson & Hedges. My mother didn't like any of it and she told her sisters that their father would kill them all if he found out. The sisters shrugged it off. They were afraid of Arthur, but not like Joanne.

One afternoon, the girls were home alone. Joanne and Martha were upstairs and Alex and Gill were sunbathing in the backyard. Joanne was drawing under the window in the bedroom, trying to tempt a breeze. Martha lit a cigarette and left Joanne alone; she knew her sister liked quiet and privacy whenever she could have it. Joanne heard Martha wander down the hall and into their parents' room where she shut the door to take a nap. She was tired from sneaking out with her boyfriend, Robbie, the night before. They'd started doing it, Martha had confessed to Joanne. Mostly in the back of Robbie's father's car, and whenever they did Martha felt sick and dizzy the next day. Her legs were all weak from holding them high with her feet pressed against the backseat windows.

Joanne kept drawing for a while. She was good in most subjects but only really enjoyed art. Time passed there under the window until a smell crept into the room. Something chemical and burning. Joanne got up and opened the bedroom door. There was smoke in the hallway.

"Martha?" she called.

She went down the hall, coughing and waving the smoke away and opened the door to their parents' room. She was met with a thick, black cloud. Then she saw the flames, licking hot at the lampshade on Diana's bedside table. Martha was sitting up in bed, coughing violently.

Joanne pulled Martha to her feet and dragged her out of the room and down the stairs. Martha leaned on Joanne for support. They burst out the front door onto the lawn and Martha collapsed, choking and spitting. Joanne ran back inside to the kitchen and filled a frying pan with water. She ran up the stairs, water slopping up onto her thighs. The fire had spread from the lampshade to the curtains. She tossed the water on the lamp, but the fire roared on. The coverlet had caught and was spreading fast, devouring the pink chintz. She didn't know fire could be so loud.

Joanne ran back downstairs. Gillian and Alexandra were with Martha on the front lawn. They were in swimsuits, faces tipped back, watching black smoke pour out of the bedroom window, rising in a stack up to the sky. Their arms were wrapped around each other. Martha was shaking. The girls stayed there frozen until, at some point, Arthur and Diana pulled up to the house in the station wagon. Diana got out of the car. She had a silk kerchief over her hair, tied in a knot under her chin. She was wearing sunglasses and her lips were painted bright red. She ran to the girls and grabbed at them.

"What happened, what happened?" she yelled, but the girls were still looking up at the smoke and the fire and they couldn't speak. Flames had spread to their room and were lapping up and out over the windowsill. My mother thought of her notebook. There was a loud crack from inside the house, the sound of wood splitting and caving in. Diana looked back to the car where Arthur was still sitting. He had both hands on the steering wheel. Diana shouted for him. He got out of the car and walked across the driveway, over the lawn and to his wife. The brim of his hat came down low in a hard line over his eyes.

"You left an ashtray burning," he said. There was only his voice, the quiet thunder of judgement.

"I'm not sure," Diana whispered.

She took a step toward Arthur, her head ducked, trying to meet his eyes.

"Please," she said.

He swung a thick arm up and ripped the kerchief roughly from her head. Diana stayed still, her lips quivering;

her stiff blond curls were ruined, broken and messy. He balled up the kerchief and threw it to the ground. He stepped toward her and ruffled her hair.

"Let everyone see your pretty hair."

He stalked away to the neighbours to call the fire department. Diana collapsed to the ground beside Martha and swung her arms around her. Martha kept coughing. Gillian and Alexandra were crying and that's when my mother felt wet between her legs. She looked down. Her knees were shaking. At some point she'd peed her pants.

My mother always believed the fire came because of her sisters. They were having sex and sneaking out and doing all of the things they'd always been told they couldn't. I don't think any amount of therapy can undo that kind of belief. You either have it or you don't. It made things hard for my mother. She behaved herself, and her sisters got over it quickly. They were excited to live in a downtown hotel while their house was being repaired. They flirted with the bellboys and snuck cocktails at the bar. Martha never confessed that it was her cigarette that started the fire. Joanne stayed up in her room and filled notebook after notebook with sketches.

Eventually, she went to McGill and studied art and met my dad. They moved away to Ontario and had me. She wanted to start over, have her own life, so she didn't baptize me or raise me with religion, but she couldn't escape those parts of her parents. Doctors explained to my dad and me over the years that psychotic insanity is caused by equal parts biological predisposition and what they call the right environment. The sisters stayed in Montreal, close to home. They got married and had babies, not always in the right order. My mother moved away and got sick. She believed in things that weren't there, she heard voices in the night.

It was hard to argue with the tidiness of the whole thing. I didn't have any proof that the devil wasn't real and our sins weren't paid back. In that way, I was pretty useless. I couldn't coax my mother out of her hiding places. She had a habit of tucking herself into corners when she was scared and unwell, beside the bed in the master bedroom, or wedged behind an armchair in the living room. Hiding from her comeuppance, like she did when she was small, under the hedges in the backyard, a pale, frightened animal with her hands in the dirt. I hated having to find her in dark rooms. I was afraid of the dark all my life. There was something deep about that fear, something primal. I didn't want to linger in those places too long.

I think she didn't baptize me because she wanted to show herself that we didn't need God. We didn't need all those things her father told her she did. That the things she believed in, that terrified her, didn't really exist.

The problem was, I was afraid too, though I could never show her that. I'd do a bad thing and wait to feel guilty, wait for fire, like my mother got, but I never did. I traded my virginity and smoked pot and stayed out late and felt nothing. I ate a fistful of shrooms with Skittles and waited to see God but didn't. Where my mother had boundaries and limits, it seemed like I had none. All those things that were bad for her were nothing to me. So maybe in that way, her experiment with me worked. We got a fresh start, without the devil. But

I felt fear. I was afraid of myself, of what I could get away with, of how far I'd go. I never felt guilt. When my mother asked me about bad things and evil and the devil, I didn't have any argument. I couldn't tell her bad things didn't exist, that everything would be okay, because who has proof of that? It's hard to argue with evil when you're terrified of being alone with yourself in the dark.

HER OWN ROOM

The delivery lights beat down hot above my mother when she gave that one last push. She felt the force of the baby's head crowning, the bloom of flesh, and the slow slide out. My father's voice felt far away, like he was in the sky. "Wow, Jo, oh she's beautiful. You did it."

They put me down, slippery and wet, on her chest. Her breasts had grown long in those last months. My mother loved to tell me this part, about how I looked up at her and my eyes were black and shiny like tadpoles. She said I looked right at her and she wanted to tuck me back up inside where I belonged.

Joanne never wanted children. She grew up with three sisters in a damp house in West Montreal. The sisters ran showers until the pipes groaned and the walls perspired. They twisted their hair up in towels and perched on the bathroom countertop with their feet in the sink. They left clothes hanging on doorknobs and banisters. Crumpled pantyhose lined the halls like snakeskin. My mother couldn't breathe in that house. She wanted fresh air. She wanted to paint in a studio with big windows and a view of the forest so she could watch the trees toss in the wind while she worked. But then she met David and she loved him. She loved to watch him read, his long fingers pressed against his temples in concentration.

David wanted a family.

I was conceived on their wedding night in the Queen Elizabeth Hotel. They got married the summer my mother was 22. They didn't know how to dance, so at the reception Joanne wrapped her arms around David's neck and put her feet on his. They turned in slow circles. David kept his lips tight in every wedding photo, his wide smile threatening to pull back with happiness and show off his braces. They left the reception early and David drove to the hotel in his father's Volvo. They ate breakfast at the hotel restaurant. Hot chocolate was served out of a silver pot. My mother never felt so free.

David finished his master's program and got a job in Toronto. They moved to a small commuter town called Milton, an hour outside the city. They moved in January and everything was icy and wet. The house was brand new: tall and thin, with a long driveway in the front.

My parents were young and beautiful, and they were finally on their own. Joanne left behind her sisters, mother, and father. She was huge with me when she unpacked boxes in the new house. She wore David's McGill hoodie and a pair of long johns while she worked. One night, after David came home from work, she was organizing the kitchen. She cleared a space at the table for him to eat. It was covered with pots and pans and Tupperware and canned food. David sat down, leafing through one of the baby name books his mother, Lorie, had sent them. Joanne got his plate from the oven. Just baked beans and grilled cheese. She set it down with a bottle of ketchup and David rolled up his sleeves.

"Oh," he said, chewing thoughtfully. "What about Naomi?"

"Naomi," my mother said.

The baby kicked out gently, into her ribs. Joanne put one hand over her belly.

"It's good," she said.

Naomi was a biblical name, something Joanne would have preferred to avoid. She would have liked something modern like Willow or Brooke or Quinn. But Naomi felt right. It had a soft sonic quality, a warmth to it that felt almost familiar.

The snow was melting when my parents brought me home from the hospital. Joanne wanted to get out of the hospital as soon as she could. She would have left right after the delivery had the nurses let her. She was sore, hadn't expected to be so sore, and she hadn't slept properly in days. She sat in the back of the car, cradling me in her arms. The car seat was up front with David. He'd installed it with care, but Joanne wanted to keep me close. She watched me with curiosity. She hadn't expected that either – to enjoy watching her baby.

She stroked my forehead with one finger. She traced my nose and I opened my mouth. It was pink. Brand new. The sun was low in the sky, casting shadows across muddy lawns. Everything was soggy.

The world felt sharp to Joanne. Some kids played hockey in a driveway. The ball against the garage made her nervous, as if all those warm windows could splinter at once, shattering into a thousand jagged pieces. Joanne held me tighter. She'd been that tired before, she'd stayed up late a few times to paint, to see how it felt, and she'd never liked it.

David's mother was at the house with dinner. Lorie was a short woman with a ski jump nose and a soft chin. She'd lived on the West Island her whole life and was excited to visit her successful son and his little wife to help with the baby. She'd gotten dressed up for the occasion and decorated the house. A banner hung in the hallway, with curly letters spelling out *It's a Girl*. Pink balloons covered the kitchen ceiling. Lorie laid dinner out with great attention: a tossed salade niçoise and three place settings with yellow paper napkins. The balloons quivered slightly with the stirring in the room, a dozen pink bellies ready to pop.

After dinner, in the bedroom, Joanne sat up against the pillows and cradled me in her arms. David got into bed beside her. David put his arm around Joanne's shoulders, and she settled back into him. This was what she had wanted, ever since the hospital. To be alone. Just the three of us.

David took a few days off from work. We stayed up in the bedroom. The first day, Joanne felt a burst of energy. "I'd like to draw," she said, and David brought her notebooks and pencils into the bed. She tried to sketch me, my forehead, my closed eyes, my hands. She propped herself up on pillows and placed me on her chest, but it was clumsy, not right. She tried and tried until she grew frustrated.

"I can't," she said.

"There's no rush," David said. He helped her put her papers aside.

For Lorie, everything was too sensitive in those days. She tried to get David and Joanne out of the bedroom. She would knock at the door and David would open it a crack. Then he'd shake his head, one finger to his lips. "We're fine," he'd whisper. "We don't need anything right now." So, Lorie bustled around downstairs and made cucumber and cream cheese sandwiches. Just how David liked when he was little. She brought plates up and Joanne and David ate in bed.

One afternoon, Lorie switched on the vacuum downstairs and Joanne woke up to my little red hands waving in the basinet. I screamed like a wounded animal. Joanne reached for me, scattering her books and loose papers, fighting off the heavy fog of sleep, calling, "No, no, don't worry," over the roar of the vacuum downstairs. David pulled the vacuum cord out of the wall. He begged Lorie to be quiet. Upstairs I cried and Joanne tried to soothe me in whispers.

"Babies cry," Lorie said.

The truth was, I cried more than other babies. I hated to be out of my mother's arms. I'd scream until my face turned red and purple. I loved my mother fiercely, selfishly; so much so that Joanne was almost afraid of me. I nursed greedily and grew fat. My mother's eyes turned dark and sharp at the edges. She watched me for hours. I was her stolen beginning, her tiny new moon. She tucked her drawing things behind the bedside table.

The first day David went back to work, Lorie put the stroller together in the front hallway. She'd brought it as a baby gift. She went upstairs and opened the bedroom door without knocking. Joanne was nursing me on the bed.

"Let's go for a little walk," Lorie said. She pulled back the curtains and Joanne winced at the light.

"Yes," said Joanne.

She was restless. A walk was a good idea. Every whimper or sigh from the bassinet set her on edge. She'd started to stay up all night while David slept, listening to me breathe in the dark. She felt nervous with exhaustion. She'd close her eyes and bright neon white shapes danced on her eyelids. She'd whisper what they looked like and try to fall asleep. A cloud, a spaceship, a dandelion scattering in the wind.

Downstairs, Joanne laid me out on the sofa and Lorie passed her little pants, sweater, and a sheepskin over suit with a fuzzy liner. Lorie reached out to help load me into the stroller, but Joanne scooped me up and put me in herself. She fumbled with the buckles and straps.

"There you go," Lorie said, as Joanne finally fastened the clip over my middle.

"It's too much," Joanne said. "I'll never get used to it."

"It just takes practice."

They set out on their walk as Lorie chatted away.

"It's a lovely neighbourhood. I hear children playing in the street after school gets out every day. If that's not good for the soul, then I don't know what is. There's nothing like the sound of children playing."

Joanne nodded. The air smelled of wet grass and mud. She was glad to be outside but everything felt cartoonish and large, as though she was a child again, reaching for the back of her mother's thick winter coat on Saint Catherine Street, the buildings impossibly tall like cliff faces, her father bouncing ahead, his hat nearly touching the sky.

They turned off their quiet street onto a busier one. A car flew by so fast Joanne had to stop from the shock of it. She felt her heart squeeze, too tight, and beat up into her throat.

"That's okay," Lorie said, her hand on Joanne's shoulder.

Another car went by, then another in the opposite direction. Joanne could feel Lorie talking to her, but all she could hear was a great white wind, the aftershock of metal and speed and heat. Lorie's hand reached out to take hold of the stroller and something in Joanne's mind clicked open like a tiny trap door. She felt a cool, wet air seep into her consciousness, something like a thought or a feeling, but closer to a voice.

The voice had all the texture of sound without any actual noise. She knew the voice was strange, dangerous even, but she was tired and afraid. The voice pushed her toward flight. It compelled her to run. She didn't think to question it.

Joanne reached down into the stroller and wrestled me up out of the straps. She held me close, her eyes wild. I started to cry.

"Joanne, dear," Lorie stammered.

My mother turned swiftly and started back for the house. Lorie followed behind her, panting and pushing the stroller. "Joanne!" she called.

With me pressed against her chest, my mother felt her heart settle back down. She wanted to zip me safely inside her coat and feel my little fingernails gripping like claws into her chest, strong enough to puncture her skin.

When David got home from work, Lorie was waiting for him.

"You know your Aunt Gail hid out in the bedroom with your cousin after he was born," she said.

"We're adjusting," David said. "She's tired. She's trying."

"You need to encourage her to get out of the house. I don't like her cooped up all day with the baby."

Lorie left the stroller set up in the front hall and Joanne ignored it. She started strapping me to her chest with a scarf. She wandered from room to room like that during the day. She never went outside.

"You'll make her fussy," Lorie warned.

But Joanne felt better when I was close. She didn't mention the voice to David. She didn't want to worry him, even though she was afraid it would come back. Her notebooks sat blank, untouched, behind the bedside table.

I cried whenever I went down in the bassinet. I screamed through the night. David would wake up and try to rock me, but I shook and bellowed until I was back in Joanne's arms. My parents grew thin.

One afternoon I was crying in the kitchen. Joanne bobbed me back and forth, but she was tired. She hadn't slept all night. David was at work and Lorie was folding laundry on the kitchen table. Lorie reached her arms out for me and took me from my mother. Joanne let go. Her arms fell heavy to her sides. It was so easy.

"Go to the store," Lorie said. "Just go."

Joanne jammed her feet into a pair of sneakers and stumbled out the front door. She found a crumpled up five in the pocket of her jacket and walked to the convenience store.

Joanne ducked inside and bought a milk chocolate bar. She chose the plainest she could find, a Cadbury without nuts or caramel. She sat down on the curb of the strip mall parking lot, peeled the wrapper open and bit into the chocolate. It was chalky and dry. It was her first time away from me since I was born. Everything felt tight, like she had a head cold. She didn't want any more crying and grabbing. She didn't want a child strapped to her side, forever needing, tugging at her sleeve, *Mommy, Mommy, now!*

Joanne saw how easy it would be to run away. How willfully forgetful the world could be. She tried to remember what it was like before I was born, why she'd gotten pregnant in the first place, but she couldn't. She remembered the feeling of the voice.

Am I going crazy? she thought. She spat a mouthful of chocolate out onto the ground. She wanted to paint. She was supposed to be painting. "Fuck," she whispered.

❖

The next day, after David went to work, Joanne got me dressed and put me into the stroller. I didn't cry.

"I'm taking her for a walk," Joanne said to Lorie.

"How nice," Lorie smiled.

She made sure we had extra layers. It was bright but cool outside. Joanne was in a hurry, the voice was pushing at her ear, tapping on the trap door, animating her limbs. Go, go.

It was windy outside. Tree branches caught in the wind and vibrated. New buds quivered, fresh in the morning light. I was awake in the stroller. Joanne didn't know where she was going, and her feet moved on their own. She turned off from our street onto the boulevard. The occasional car sped past us, but the noise didn't bother her that day. The cars rushed north toward the grocery store or the highway. Open fields and bungalows. Old barns rotted and collapsed in on themselves.

Joanne walked along the boulevard until she got to the bridge. It passed over the deepest part of the ravine, where the trees fell away sharply on either side. A creek flowed underneath, and a paved path led away from the sidewalk, sloping down far below the bridge where a signpost and small map sat beside the creek to mark gravel trails. It was dark there, shaded by the bridge and thick trees. Joanne rolled me to the top of the path. It was a long, steep way down to the map and trails.

Joanne hovered where the path poured away from the sidewalk and the trapdoor opened again. A few cars passed over the bridge and the rumble of traffic echoed into the forest below. In that roar, Joanne could hear the brutal footfalls of eternity. She could hear the tired steps of all those women who had gone before her. She was caught. Like she'd been blindfolded and spun around fast at a party. Pin the tail on the donkey!

Joanne lurched forward and her grip loosened on the stroller. She was ready to let go, let everything coast down into the dark. The voice was with her, willing her fingers to unfurl, to be free of me. One by one, they started to come open, like buttons on a heavy wool sweater.

Then a sound came from the stroller. Not a cry or a gurgle. It was more like a moan, a little cloud of breath. Something like a word like, my name, Naomi, or maybe Mommy.

Joanne tightened her grip. She peered down. I met her gaze with dark eyes, shiny and wet with life.

When Joanne got home, we both fell fast asleep. Joanne didn't dream. When she woke up it was dark, and David was home, watching us.

"Come here," he whispered to Joanne. "I want to show you something."

He led her out into the upstairs hallway and to the linen closet. He pulled the chain for the bulb and the light flickered on. He had a ladder propped up at the back of the closet.

"It's big up there." He pointed to the ceiling.

The attic door was open. David was grinning, excited. Joanne saw it then; how happy he really was.

"Go on," he said. "It's for you."

Joanne climbed up the ladder into the attic. There was a high, pitched ceiling and a small circular window at the far end. It was a clear night and the moon was nearly full, letting in enough light to bathe the room in a milky blue glow.

David climbed up after Joanne and dusted his hands on his pants.

"I was thinking, a studio? I'd want to make that whole wall a window."

He strode toward the far wall and peered out into the night. Joanne followed him. The window looked out over the forest; the treetops were still.

"It's perfect," she said.

It wouldn't be the same as anything that came before. She saw that then. It would be their own life. Their unhappiness would be their own, their happiness too. She thought about telling David about the voice, but he reached for her, so happy and pulled her close. The next day she'd draw. She was nearly ready to try again.

HABIT BREAKER

Joanne was sitting on a bench in town watching the street. She wore black sunglasses and a wide, beachy hat. She sat with her hands resting palms up, adopting the pose of New-Age prayer, not because she knew much about prayer outside of Catholic recitation but because it brought her a sense of connectedness to everything that pulsed around her, from the blushing red skin of a newborn in a stroller to the ringing of brass church bells down the block, striking noon with all the miraculous clarity of thunder and lightning. She could feel the baby's breath on her fingertips, the hum of the bells in her knuckle-bones.

My mother wanted to start over. She wouldn't have said so because she didn't think of it that way. She would have said she waiting to be reborn. Her life as a mother had come to an end. Her marriage, too. It was like she'd built a house for her family on a frozen lake, and finally the ice had broken up beneath it. It wasn't because of anything anyone did. It was just a new season rolling in. My father and I were gone, sunk down in green water.

She'd been in bed for weeks. I was freshly 18, long-legged and clever, puttering noisily around the house after my father left. I had no plans for adulthood and Joanne wanted to be alone, to be rid of me. She felt that it was time. So, she hid in bed and fasted everything out of her system, including the pills that kept her sane. She lost weight and melted into the mattress until her mind cracked open and bled gold like a fresh egg. When it did, she got out of bed and got dressed. She slung heavy silver bangles up her right arm and left her other arm bare. Her shoulder blades itched like they might sprout wings. She'd better stay thin, she thought, in case she needed to fly.

She wrapped herself in a crocheted shawl and got in the Volvo. She drove down to the waterfront, where there was an old-fashioned stretch of shops and restaurants by the lake marina. It was sleepy and pretty and had a small-town Americana thing about it that she'd always liked, although she'd never spent much time in that part of town. Joanne was an artist and she wasn't meant for small towns or shopping or going to the bank.

But that day she felt that she should to be close to the movements of normal people, of everyday life. At times like that, my mother was quite vulnerable. It's hard to explain. She never planned to go missing, but Joanne wasn't used to planning anything anymore. Her days were unstructured, based off of feelings, pushes and pulls. She was there, but everything seemed to happen *to* her, not *because of* her, like a complicated dream with moving passages and staircases that unfolded and stretched long like paper pop-up books. When she was like that, people were drawn to her, by instinct; they could sense a certain kind of madness, feel that she was on shaky ground. It was easy for things to happen to her, all of a sudden.

That is why a man named Ted sat down beside my mother, beautiful, enigmatic, alone, and vibrating with such intensity. He sniffed her out like a lumbering bear, like she was a hive dripping with honey.

"Hello," he said.

My mother tipped her head back so she could see her visitor from under the brim of her hat. He was a large, growly man with an unlit cigarillo stuck between his teeth.

"Hello," she cooed.

"Do you mind?" He held a lighter up.

She shook her head.

Ted introduced himself and chatted her up, inconspicuously, like an older man on a bench just might. He asked her about her line of work.

"Yes, you look like an artist."

"Thank you."

"Where did you grow up?"

"Montreal."

"I have cousins there. But you wouldn't know them. Criminals, all of them."

My mother wasn't much of a talker, even when her mind was starting to gush and spill over with affection for all things, from a car revving with life to Ted's massive knees, knotted thick as cinder blocks.

"Is your work here? In the galleries?" Ted gestured up and down the street with his cigarillo.

"No, not here."

"In the city, I bet. Well, there's more money there, that's for sure. More art collector types, I bet."

They sat and he smoked. My mother clenched her palms into little fists and then opened them again, feeling the tiny muscles in her pinky fingers flush hot with blood. She glanced at Ted's hands. Strong and muscled. Worn, like an old leather saddle. How alike all things were, she thought. All flesh is the same, all muscles and neurons like grand celestial bodies, scattered in the dark night. She was used to feeling like magic, a bit, under the surface of thought but never did she let herself touch it, feel the texture of life. Off her meds, Joanne was tipping ecstatically into something more like madness and less like artistry. The lines between such things only seem murky when people are between them, with a foot in each world, as Joanne was then, sitting beside Ted on the bench.

She believed in rebirth, but in that moment, she believed in sex more. As a possible mover, a kind of impetus for change. Sex could be a vehicle for great thought, she always felt. Alone, she was inert.

"Do you want to have supper?" she asked.

"Sure," Ted said.

They went to an all-day diner. Ted ordered steak and eggs. My mother got eggs florentine with sliced tomatoes. They poured Chardonnay from a glass jug.

"You should always get everything well done," Ted said when my mother's eggs arrived runny.

Her back itched again. She wouldn't eat, she didn't want to become heavy, weighted. She wanted to fly. Ted cleared his plate and then hers. Under the harsh lights of the diner she could see his gums were receding. Ted reached across the table for my mother's hand and she felt a great chill. She shouldn't be there. Then she thought of Ted thrusting on top of her, crushing her wing buds.

She got the bill and paid in a rush, stumbling outside, Ted on her heels.

"Wait up," he said.

It was dark and the sun had set. Old-fashioned gas lamps lit up the streets. Joanne said goodnight and tried to bolt away from Ted, but he reached for her forearm and pulled her back. He tried to kiss her, but Joanne spat at him on an impulse. It shot out in every direction, on his chin and chest.

"What the fuck?"

She laughed and took off. She could hear him shouting after her, but she felt like a child, her feet were so light, like she was trying to shake off her shadow. She ran and ran back to her parking spot by the marina. She stopped, panting, and dug for her keys in her bag.

She drove, but not home. She went north.

Sex was a diversion, she thought as she drove. A misplaced energy. She needed to focus on flight. She drove steadily in the dark, into the countryside, past little houses set back from the road, their little windows twinkling with white light. She drove until she got to Lake Simcoe. She pulled off along the lakeside road and parked the car. She rolled her window down, sniffing the lake water air. It was late and she booked herself into the first motel she came across. It was a low, long brown brick building across the street from a beachside park. She always liked arriving in new places at night in the dark because everything stayed a mystery until morning. She had to ring a bell at the front desk so a lady would come. In her room, she shook a black silk scarf out from the bottom of her bag and draped it over the bedside table lamp. It cast the room in a hazy grey. Joanne wanted to be wild. She walked along the beach in the dark and pulled her shawl tight around her shoulders. It was chilly and she wasn't tired, not at all.

Some teenagers were having a bonfire. Joanne could smell pot. She'd only smoked once or twice with her agent and my dad late at night in the house when I was little and asleep. It made her feel fast and clever. It made strange connections fire rapidly in her brain while symbols carved themselves in neon light on her closed eyelids. She walked into the bonfire's ring of light.

"Do any of you have some pot?"

The circle fell silent. Someone laughed nervously. Joanne raised her chin but kept her eyes cast down. She remembered reading that body language spoke to teenagers. Their frontal lobes were underdeveloped; they were closer to beasts than to humans, really. So she kept her chin up, but she couldn't bring herself to look at them. They were too much like me and she didn't want to think about me alone in the house just yet.

One boy got up from the circle and held out his hand to Joanne. It was a joint. She peeled a bill out of her purse and handed it to him. He took it.

"I need a lighter," Joanne said.

The boy dug in his pocket and lit up for her. He exhaled smoke up over her head. Joanne closed her eyes and felt the smoke swirl around her shoulders.

Joanne took the lit joint and walked back the way she'd come. She coughed her way through and buried what was left of it in the sand. Her tongue itched and then tingled, and the feeling spread to her lips and gums. She couldn't feel her teeth.

She watched the sun come up and she wished she had a set of watercolours.

Joanne went back to her motel room, found paper and a pen, and sat up on the bed trying to recreate the lines of the morning sky over and over until the pad ran out. She got under the covers and closed her eyes, but her mind clicked away with the compulsive rhythm of a clock. What a waste, living all that time away from a body of water. What a waste, all that time, not smoking and scooping up fistfuls of sand, every bead touching her fingers, kissing her with their presence, hello, hello, we're all here. She'd invested so much of herself in the routines of motherhood, of setting the day up right. Boiling eggs, one mashed up for the baby and one for herself, the pieces of shell sticking to the countertop like candy sprinkles. None of that mattered. She'd believed too much when the doctor and my father said she had to take the medication in order to be well. She realized then, that she hadn't felt like herself in years, not really. She was coming back, coming up for air like a cetacean. She was Joanne again. She'd forgotten, that entire time, about energy, about the stars and her breath fogging up a spoon at the dinner table, her feet swinging high up because she was too small to touch the ground. She remembered reading something, somewhere, about a car accident being sucked into a sinkhole and how that could be reversed. She felt like she had been alive forever and never all at the same time. She felt, more than ever, that she was close to rebirth and she had to go to the water to wait for it to happen. Her wing buds itched. If it was going to come, it would come at the water.

Joanne kicked back the blankets and got her purse. She locked the motel room door. The parks along the beach were alive with people. They were setting up blankets and coolers. Maybe it was a Saturday. Joanne walked fast toward a little cluster of shops. There was a Big Bee, a liquor store, and a dollar store. She found a simple watercolour set and some oil pastels. She got a big pad of white paper, a chocolate bar from the rack at the cash, and three litres of bottled water.

She carried her plastic bags back toward a park near the motel. She spread her shawl out on the ground and took out her paints and pastels. Joanne started to paint the lake. The air was crisp, not too cool. It was a perfect day. She drank water. She didn't notice the line of dirt under her nails from the sand the night before. She wasn't hungry so she opened her chocolate bar just to watch it melt in a patch of sunlight. There was a big group in the park at the barbecues. They were grilling meat. Joanne kept her head down and switched to pastels. She ripped page after page out of her pad and anchored them around her in a circle with rocks and sticks.

Some of the kids from the barbecues came over to her. They stared curiously from behind wide oak trees. A brave little one wandered close and stood behind Joanne.

"What are you doing?" he asked.

Joanne held up her landscape so he could see. It was pink and orange, a bit off, somehow, the perspective was incorrect.

The boy took a step closer and a mother's worried voice rose from the group. "Joshua! Come here!"

"That's my mom," the boy said. He ran off back to the group.

Joanne stayed in the park all day. The families started to clear out. They loaded their coolers and kids into their minivans. The sun shifted overhead. Joanne used the heel of her palm to blend blue and green over a fresh page. Another group took over the picnic benches and the barbecues. The sun started to set. Joanne's head felt tight, like a balloon about to pop. Everything seemed to accelerate and narrow. There was a long, low whistle from the picnic tables. Joanne ignored it. She lay back in the grass and tucked her hands under her head. She closed her eyes and felt her back settle into the earth, as if her wing buds were sending down roots, not growing feathers, but anchoring her to the planet. Spinning there on a rock in the infinite black sky, to Joanne, it felt like flying.

"Hello," a voice said from above her.

Joanne opened her eyes. A woman stood peering over her under the shade of the tree.

"We saw you were alone. Do you want to join us?"

She was a tiny thing. Dark hair and big black eyes. She had a bottle tucked under her arm. Joanne sat up and stared at the woman. She had thin, black etchings: tattoos that stretched from her wrists, up her arms, under her T-shirt sleeves and all the way to her neck. She was wrinkled around the eyes, but she smiled and Joanne trusted her at once. She sat up and the woman helped her stand.

"Thank you," Joanne said.

The woman pointed down at the drawings.

"Let me help you," she said.

They both got down on their knees and swept all of the pages up into a stack. The pages were wrinkled and warped, dry from the paint and heavy with oil pastels.

"These are beautiful," the woman said.

"I'm an artist," Joanne said.

The woman nodded.

"My name's Victory."

"I'm Joanne."

They arranged the pages carefully into plastic bags.

Victory linked her arm through Joanne's and led her across the park to the group at the tables.

Victory announced Joanne. There were four men. They didn't say their names, just nodded and said hello. Victory handed Joanne the bottle. Joanne sat on top of a table with her feet on the bench. She kept her bags of drawings on her lap. She felt they were important, somehow, that they'd help her tell a story later of how she managed to start over, to find rebirth. She drank from the bottle. The liquor was brown and burned her throat. One of the men had a guitar and started to play. Victory sang along. She had a beautiful voice, rough and heartbreaking. Joanne wanted her to sing all night. They drank and Joanne sat quietly in the group. It got dark and they built a fire in one of the barbecues and let it burn high.

Victory went off with one of the men for a while, so it was quiet except for the men talking. Joanne realized she couldn't understand what they were saying. She knew they were speaking and she could make out a couple of words, but she was having trouble connecting them. She hadn't slept in so long. A joint got passed around. Joanne felt dizzy and wanted to stand, so she tried but stumbled forward and one of the bags fell from her lap. Blue and green and purple pages spilled forward onto the ground. Joanne scrambled after them as a wind picked up and blew them around. She got on all fours and scraped them over the ground. Her bangles clattered sharply. The pages were dirty. The man with the guitar got up and tried to help her, but Joanne was moving too fast, grabbing the pages and crumpling them because she was being careless, and she felt it, that she wasn't in touch with the earth or the trees anymore. She didn't feel like wings couldn't grow on her back anymore. She saw one painting as she picked it up and the lines were all wrong, the proportions of the sky to the lake bent impossibly at a strange angle. They were idiotic pictures, unsophisticated. There was no grand connection. In the light of the fire, her hands were streaked with dirt and pastels. She was dirty, all used up.

"Hey," the guitar man said. "Are you okay?"

Joanne bundled up her pictures and left the fire. The man followed her to the road. They walked side by side. Every step felt like forever, she felt it in her bones the way old people feel rain and bad weather. Now and then her shoulders shook with a dry sob or a moan. She didn't feel those sounds in her head, just heard them echoing far away, like an animal dying on the beach. At the motel, Joanne let the man inside after her.

She made him leave that night. He stood at the door and called her baby. He tucked her hair behind her ear. She leaned her chin into his palm, and it would have been so easy to keep him for a little while longer. But Joanne gave up and the man left angry.

She kept all the lights off and drew the red floral curtains tight. She turned down the sheets and lay in the middle of the bed with all her limbs stretched out like a dead body. She couldn't stay up any longer. She slept and slept and when she woke up it was night again. Her eyes were cloudy and heavy. She checked out of the motel and drove with the paintings in plastic bags on the passenger seat beside her. She drove south and stopped at a roadside restaurant for a chicken dinner. She couldn't eat any of it. Its wing bone was fried; its skin crispy and melted, stuck to its side. She'd never fly or lose her shadow or fall in love again. She got back in the car and drove without a direction.

THE LEAVING TIME

The ER wasn't busy that night. I sat with my mother in a row of stiff-backed chairs. The ceiling above us was water-stained and brown.

The only other patient in the waiting room was sitting at the check-in desk. The nurse motioned to him from behind the protective glass and he leaned forward, arms crossed over his stomach.

"September the ninth, 1988?" the nurse asked.

"Yeah," the man said.

He groaned and the nurse typed on the keyboard. The room smelled sharp, like a concoction of pine needles and rubbing alcohol, and the chair legs were all smudged and dirty. Doorways and walls were spotted with hundreds of grey fingerprints.

"How are you feeling?" I asked my mother.

Her eyes were tight and anguished. They darted back and forth. I'd found her earlier that night, dirty and unslept in a chair at home. Thick dandruff had settled on her shoulders like frost. All the bones in her chest stuck out under her skin. She was so small and grey that I'd almost hadn't see her there in the dark.

"My heart is squeezing," she whispered.

"What are you thinking about?"

She looked down at the floor and nodded her head, listening to something else, some voice I couldn't hear.

I took one of my mother's hands. A triage nurse had bandaged them up. Her fingers stuck out of the white gauze, five little girls in red berets standing deep in snow. Under the bandages her palms were split, the skin bloody and broken. At the house, I'd helped her up from the chair and tried to get her to the kitchen to eat something. She'd smashed a picture in the hallway, reaching up and slapping the hanging frame flat with her palm. The glass had shattered and fallen to the floor. *Stop it!* she'd cried at the photo, a picture of her from years ago. In it she wore a denim cap and bathing suit, and she was smiling at the camera, at my father on the other side of the lens. She'd bent over to pick up the pieces of glass and blood fell from her palms in fat, red drops. She'd fumbled a piece of glass and sliced her other hand clean open.

I'd said, I think we need to go to the hospital now, Mom.

And she'd said, oh yes. I've hurt myself.

The man at the check-in desk got up and struggled toward a chair. He sat down with a hard sigh and the nurse kept typing at the keyboard.

My mother looked up from the floor at the man. A baby cried down the hallway, a tiny yowl like a kitten.

"A baby," my mother said.

"Yes," I said.

We sat and waited, and the man shifted and moaned. I held on to my mother's bandaged hand. I was well past true exhaustion: every ping and click in the room sent me reeling. Even if I'd had the opportunity to sleep, I don't think I could have. My legs twitched. I felt like running. I bit my bottom lip.

"When you were little," my mother said, "we had to take you back to the hospital."

She looked closely at me, her eyes steady on my neck and ear. I knew the story well. I wanted to keep her talking about real things, things that had happened.

"Tell me," I said.

"Two months," she said. "So little."

She let go of my hand and started to fumble with her paper hospital bracelet. It rubbed roughly over her skin.

"I hated the hospital when you were born," she said. "But you were fussy all day."

The man whined in his seat and gasped. He leaned forward, still clutching his stomach.

"Something wasn't right," my mother said. "I was breast-feeding, and I didn't know what to do. So, when your father came home from work, I said: 'We have to go, we have to take her to the emergency.'"

"Nurse," the man said hoarsely. "Nurse."

I craned my neck to see what was happening.

"The first time they took your temperature it was fine, normal."

"Help," the man said. He started to cough.

"Then the second time you had a fever."

The man coughed harder and stood up. He bent over and retched.

I jumped up out of my chair and called to the nurse across the room. "Excuse me."

She looked up; her eyes fixed on the glass in front of her.

"He needs some help," I said.

The nurse left one hand on the keyboard and pointed past me with the other. "Miss, sit down," she said.

My mother stopped twisting her hospital bracelet and watched the man cough. He retched again and threw up on the floor. A stink like hot milk filled the room. I sat down.

Two double doors to the emergency wing opened and another nurse came out. She was wearing yellow scrubs. She took the man by the arm.

"Here, now, sit back," she said.

She called for an orderly and the man sputtered and retched.

"You're all right, you're all right," she said.

An orderly in a maroon uniform came with a mop and bucket. He was huge, his forearms. The nurse checked the man's temperature and then disappeared back into the wing.

"I think I should speak to him," my mother said. She pointed one gauze-wrapped hand at the sick man.

"No, Mom," I said. "Stay here with me."

The orderly wrung out the mop and slapped it onto the floor, struggling to work it over his belly, hanging in a low flap over his waistband.

The nurse came back with a pan and a cup of ice chips. She set the pan down on the wet floor and handed the cup to the coughing man. The orderly wrung the mop out again and slopped it onto the floor. He wheezed. When he was done, he pushed the bucket away, down the hall and out of the ER. The nurse in the yellow scrubs went back into the wing.

My mother settled both hands in her lap. "He's talking to me," she said.

"No, Mom."

I leaned forward in my seat and rubbed my eyes. It was getting late. I was so tired. I'd messed up somehow, done too much back and forth from my apartment to her house these last few years. She needed more care, more oversight. I should have admitted that. There was something about the way she went off her meds; the way she lost her mind intentionally.

Sometimes she'd become all the best parts of herself, brilliant and glamorous, for a little while. But then she'd change – she always did – and slip into something more like desperation, as if she were dying. She'd start to believe things that weren't real, like that she'd been an angel in a past life and that the devil was coming for her. Usually she'd get scared and it was easy to talk her into taking her medication again. But that last time, I hadn't done enough. I'd been distracted, I'd been distant. And now, she was too far away from me.

"He wants to be healed," she whispered to me. "I can heal him."

"No," I said.

Since we'd been on our own, without my dad, I'd managed okay. I'd kept her clean and fed and most of all, out of the hospital. But now her illness was deep in her brain, moving her lips too fast. In the living room, when I'd found her, she'd chattered to me about the apocalypse: hot, embered skies and rain-fire. Then she'd smashed the picture.

The problem was I wanted to be alone. I wanted to stay up all night and hold down a shitty job and make rent and fuck and drink and fall in love and be reckless and stupid. I had to be away from her to do all those things. With her, I couldn't have my own secrets. She'd see them in me, know them from the way I paused mid-sentence or tucked my hair behind my ear. She knew me deeply, too much. She loved me with her whole body. I loved her with my stomach. Sometimes it made me feel sick.

The doors to the wing opened again. The nurse in the yellow scrubs stood with a file folder and called my mother's name. We stood up and crossed the room, passing by the sick man. He was crumpled over in his chair. He looked up at me, his face pale and shiny with sweat, and his eyes were dull and placid, like a cow.

"This way," the nurse said. She waved us closer with a long arm. Her nails were glossy and pink, filed into sharp points. She hit a red security button on the wall and the doors shut behind us.

The nurse's station was in the middle of the wing. It was piled with folders. White and blue curtains separated the examination areas. I sensed there were people there in the wing, behind those curtains, but it was quiet except for the beeps from unseen machinery.

The nurse held my mother's chart. She checked it, paused for a minute and then looked back at us.

"Okay," she said. "Follow me."

She led us through the wing and down a side hall. She opened a wide, blue door with a small window and held it open for us. It was a square room. Everything in the room was blue. The floor was rubber, speckled with silver reflective bits. There was a chair with a navy cushion and wooden legs.

"Have a seat," the nurse said.

My mother stared at the chair, then at me. Unsure.

"Here," I said.

I put my hand on her back and steered her into the chair. She sat.

"I have to lock you in," the nurse said.

I wheeled around. "What?"

"Do you want to wait with her?"

The baby cried. It was louder now, coming from somewhere in the wing.

"Yes," I said. "I'll wait with her."

"Then I'll have to lock you in," the nurse repeated. "It will be just a minute."

She stepped back out of the room and shut the door. A key turned in the lock and the bolt clicked. I went to the door and peered through the window out into the hall. Protective wire ran through the pane in a grid. The baby cried and cried.

"Just like you," my mother said.

Her voice was light, afraid. Her eyes moved quickly. "No one knew what to do with you," my mother said. "You had such a fever. You were burning up."

The hallway was deserted. I pushed on the door, just in case, but it didn't budge. My mother started to murmur to herself. She was speaking too softly for me to hear what she was saying, but her tone felt pernicious, like she was setting a curse. I moved closer to the window, my cheek touching the pane, and I tried to see around the corner of the hall. I had to flag down an orderly or nurse. I thought maybe they had forgotten us already and we would be in that blue room all night. Stuck alone with my mother, she, and her illness, would finally absorb me. That was where I belonged, I knew, tucked in warmly at her side, but the thought scared me. I'd always known that I was hers, a kind of animal knowledge like how cats knew to hide from earthquakes. I knew it before time or place or even my own name. But her mind was bigger than me; she needed me. I knew I might never be away from her.

A woman came around the corner of the hall. She was wearing baggy exercise pants and a sweatshirt, striding briskly with a clipboard tucked in the crook of one arm. Her hair was in a ponytail. She met my eyes right away and I saw that she had a key in her hand. She nodded at me and unlocked the door. I stepped back into the room and she came inside.

"Hello," she said.

She left the door open behind her. My mother stopped murmuring. Some part of her understood that this woman was a medical authority. Some part of her was still in the room with me.

"My name is Alexa," the woman said. "I'm a social worker. Who is Joanne?"

"That's my mom," I said. I went and stood beside her.

Alexa nodded. She had brown bangs that curled under across her forehead. She was neat; her nails were trimmed short and clean, her skin was smooth, relaxed, and her mouth was neutral. It didn't fall, out of habit like most people's, into a frown. The sleeves of her sweatshirt were cuffed over.

"I hurt my hands," my mother said. She held them up, bandaged palms flat to the ceiling.

Alexa nodded. She looked at me and smiled.

"Let me get you a seat," she said.

She left the room and came back with another blue padded chair. Alexa placed the chair beside my mother, and I sat down.

"Joanne, how did you hurt your hands?" she asked.

"I smashed a picture."

My mother furrowed her brow.

"That's okay," Alexa said.

"This sense of dread," my mother shivered. "It comes over me and I can't move."

Alexa nodded and wrote something on her clipboard.

"Do you know where you are?" Alexa said.

My mother looked at her hands. "The hospital."

"Do you know the name of this hospital?"

She looked up at me and opened her mouth. Then she closed it tight.

"That's okay," Alexa said. "Do you know what day it is?"

My mother looked at me and watched my chin.

"You were so little," she said.

There was a stray hair hanging in front of her face. I pushed it back behind her ear.

"She's hearing voices," I said. "She's usually on Risperdal, but she stopped."

Alexa looked down at her clipboard, scanning the medical history and list of medications I'd supplied at the check-in desk.

"Okay," Alexa said. "Joanne, I need to speak to your daughter for a minute. We'll be right back."

She went out into the hall.

"I'll be back in a minute, Mom," I said.

I felt the guilty thrill of leaving her. How easy it would have been to walk away. The hallway seemed to stretch, pull away, on forever. The ceiling lights went back in a long, raw, horror film-like line, deep into the hospital. I didn't know which way was out. I hadn't realized how big the building was.

"Naomi," Alexa said.

Up close I could see she was only a few years older than me. I felt embarrassed; self-conscious at how I'd let my mother get sick.

"A doctor from psych is going to come down in the morning and see your mother," Alexa said. "They will issue a form on her. That means we are going to transfer her up and keep her for an observation period."

"Okay," I said.

"She's been in the hospital before," Alexa said.

"Yeah," I said. "When I was younger."

"I'll walk you through the intake process. It's likely she'll have to stay for a few weeks."

"Where will she stay?"

"In the psychiatric ward."

"Okay," I said.

I looked back down the hall at the track of lights. They extended deep into the hospital. I didn't want to leave her in this place.

"I haven't done this before," I said.

Alexa held the clipboard against her chest.

"Psych patients who routinely go off their meds often need extra care. We'll have to get her to stable. How is she taking care of herself?"

"She's not, really."

"Showering, eating, that kind of thing?"

"I don't think so."

"Do you have anyone else to help out?"

"My dad – her ex – and his girlfriend. They're supportive."

"It might be good to reach out. Even just for you. I'm going to get her a gown. I'll be right back."

I went back into the blue room and sat down beside my mother. She was whispering to herself again. I took her hand. My dad and Renata appreciated updates and would have been more involved had my mother not insisted otherwise. We're fine, just us, aren't we? she always said. And I wanted us to be; I wanted to be enough. I hadn't called my dad in a while, hadn't responded to his messages. I bit hard into my lip and it started to bleed. I wiped it with the back of my hand. I had to stop doing that. All that cellular regeneration. I'd get cancer for sure. I couldn't remember the time difference in Winnipeg. Were they asleep? Renata would answer, she always did, her voice upbeat at any hour, rousing my dad in the bed beside her. The sheets would rustle against the speaker while she passed me over to him, David, David, it's Naomi. The thought of their bare legs intertwined made my chest ache.

I watched my mother. Her bandaged hands, her worried blue eyes. She was staring at the floor again, murmuring to herself. I was supposed to take her to the hospital, but I couldn't leave her there in the room with the locked door and the cage wire glass. With the dirty walls and the man throwing up on the floor. I thought, for a second, about leaving with her, running hand in hand down the hall.

"Who was that girl?" my mother said.

"A social worker," I said.

Alexa came back, wheeling a gurney piled with blue and white linens into the room. She shut the door behind her and unfolded the sheets, making up a bed.

"That's a bit more comfortable than the chair," she said.

She patted the top with one hand, smoothing the wrinkles out of the sheets. She turned to my mother.

"I'm going to help you get changed," she said. "Why don't you come up on the bed."

My mother climbed onto the gurney like a small child, feet over hands. She let Alexa help her out of her clothes, bending her arms in like sinewy wings. The gurney squeaked under her.

"There," Alexa said.

She had tied two gowns over my mother's front and back to make a kind of dress. Alexa folded my mother's clothes up and put them in a plastic bag.

"We'll keep track of these for you," she said.

My mother let her feet dangle over the floor. They were impossibly small. I remembered playing dress up with her things in the front hall closet, with her boots and trench coat. How big those things felt on me. All I ever wanted was to be like her. To inhale her smell on her clothes and crawl into bed with her at night. When I was little I told her, "Mommy when you die, I'll die too." She laughed until she cried. I remember that part. How it felt silly at first and then like I'd done something to hurt her on purpose.

"I'll be back to check on you soon," Alexa said. "I need to file our intake with psych."

"Okay," I said.

Alexa slipped out of the room, leaving the door open again. My mother stared at the blue wall across from her. The gown was tied firmly over her back, held in place by green strings. Alexa had looped them into neat bows. I straightened the sleeves of the gown and pulled them crisp to my mother's wrists.

"Mom," I said, "what happened to me when I was little?"

She didn't answer right away. She hummed a bit to herself and rocked back and forth. The sound was thick like a lullaby.

"Mom?"

The wing was quiet. My mother rubbed one eye with the tip of her finger. I could smell the linens, clean like bar soap.

"They helped us," she said. "And when we took you home, you were better."

I didn't know whether to stay or leave. I hadn't decided. yet. The truth is, leaving is impossible, and staying is too. You never know what to do. So I decided to stay, just for a little while longer, just until I was ready to make up my mind.

X

M^ARCE

SOME KIND OF GONE

I met Marce the summer after my parents split. I'd just finished high school and I had no plans about my future or a career. Those expectations kind of drifted to the wayside the last year we were a proper family, and my dad would say stuff like, "Just be well, no matter what, take care of yourself. I love you no matter what." The bar was set pretty low.

My dad moved out shortly after my graduation. I remember how he sat with my mom at the ceremony holding her hand, whispering encouraging words to her. Joanne wore sunglasses the whole time even though the thing was in the gym. She'd only go out if my dad was there at her side and she had the right dose of lorazepam in her system. I couldn't blame him for leaving. He hadn't had much peace since my mother got really odd, really housebound, sick and afraid, and while she was in regular therapy, on regular antipsychotics, and still painting and selling reasonably well. She was different, very peculiar, and he took care of her. He got skinny and nervous and tried to keep her afloat, while she asked him, again and again, to leave her alone, to please go away, so they could both finally be free to find their soulmates.

One summer night, when I got home from my job at the mall and found the Volvo missing from the driveway and the house empty, it was obvious something was off. David, of course, wasn't there, and my mother hadn't left the house in weeks. In retrospect, I like to think of that particular disappearance as happening slowly, in minor increments, a snowball gathering steady speed downhill before becoming a boulder and crashing squarely at my feet. After my graduation, she'd hid out in the dark corners of the living room and the master bedroom. She'd stay in bed until the sheets went sour. And then, like a magician's final trick, she was gone.

I did a quick search of the house. The drawers in her room were all open, clothes had been tossed out and left in piles on the floor, but she hadn't taken anything. She hadn't left a note scribbled and stuck to the fridge. She'd left in a hurry, perhaps not to miss out on a sudden surge of energy. She had to capitalize on motivation like that. It was rare.

I had a shower and drank some orange juice straight from the carton. I could feel the echo of her voice, hoarse from too much sleep, still reverberating through the house. Her smell lingered on the furniture, in the bathroom, the kitchen. Her slippers sat, heels together in front of the sink, alone in the dark. The strange finality of her absence was what shocked me the most, how easy it was for her to disappear. And then, how little I cared, how relieved I was to be rid of her. I left the orange juice on the counter and went out.

I walked down the boulevard to a house where I knew people would be partying. Two brothers lived there. I knew them from junior school. They put out word whenever their parents were away. They used to snort Pixy Stix in the back of class to mess with supply teachers. Their noses would pour blood and they'd throw themselves on the floor in convulsions.

It was dark, but the roads were lit up, all red and yellow from passing cars. I was tired from work; my ears were ringing. It was a retail job, a lot of standing and smiling and folding thin, neon shirts into pretty little squares. They played the music loud and we had to wear these earpiece walkie-talkies even though we only ever used them to complain about customers being dicks. *Copy that. A class one a-hole headed toward denim, over.*

I came to the end of the boys' street. You could hear the rumble of bass from six houses down. Cars were packed into the driveway and all the lights in the house were on. Bodies pressed against every window.

There was a group on the front porch smoking, their voices carrying upward into the night. I sat down on the curb in front of the house. The music changed inside and the windowpanes rattled. The smokers were talking on the porch, but I couldn't make out what they were saying over the music. I wasn't ready to go in. There were some little kids on the other side of the street, all standing in a huddle near a red fire hydrant. They had their feet thrust in the middle of a circle and one kid was on his knees doing eeny, meeny, miny, moe, tapping on their sneakers. They were about to play tag.

I lit up a cigarette. I wasn't much of a smoker; mostly I held them to look busy, like I had something to do on my break at work. I tried to picture my mother driving alone in the dark. I wouldn't call my dad. That wouldn't be the right thing to do. He needed some peace. I wanted him to be away. That's what I said to him, when they decided. Maybe you should try living apart. It would be good for him. He'd meet someone a bit more balanced. That helped as much as it hurt.

One of the little kids across the street shouted and all of them scattered, breaking the circle, so one was left with his hands over his eyes, counting. One, two, three. When was the last time I went out to play? Was there a last time? If there was, my mother would have sensed it. She was always around, peeking through curtains. Watching me run. She was always afraid. Sometimes I'd come in after a long day of tag and make believe and she'd want to hear everything, from start to finish.

A car pulled up in front of the house. A girl was yelling inside, thrashing in the passenger seat. She swung the door open and her voice carried into the night.

"Oh, fuck you, you fuck."

She got out, untwining two long legs. She slammed the door and stomped across to the house. The car crept forward and pulled over, parking a little way down the street.

The girl swung a heavy purse over her shoulder, crossed her arms and headed toward the curb. She wobbled on thin heels, taking long careless strides. She tossed her bag onto the grass and crumpled to the curb.

The driver cut the engine and got out. He was tall, wearing a T-shirt and ballcap. He locked the car and jiggled the handle, walking along the road, past me and then the girl, before he turned up the driveway and went into the house.

"Shithead," the girl hissed. She ran her hands through her hair. She was wearing a thin pair of gold earrings that brushed her shoulders. She went to work unstrapping her shoes and then tossed them over her shoulder beside her purse. Then she turned to me.

"Can I bum a smoke?"

"Sure."

"Thanks."

I passed her the pack, reaching a full arm's length toward her. She put a cigarette between her lips and then tossed the pack back to me. I fumbled it in my lap. She dug her fingers into her front pocket and pulled out a lighter. She lit up, the flame glowing inches from her face. Her fingernails were bitten down and painted cherry red.

"That guy's a tool," the girl said with the cigarette in her mouth.

I shrugged, ashing on the road.

"He wants to get fucked up tonight. Do you know these people?" She waved back at the house.

"Not really," I said.

"I hate parties, people measuring each other up. He's supposed to be my ride downtown. Not my boyfriend, way too flippant. Fuck, I hate flippant people. Like, if you want to do something, commit to it, just do it."

The girl spoke with the rhythmic assurance, the measured beat of someone who was used to filling the air with her voice. I propped my elbow up on my knee and rested my chin in my palm. I already liked her. She had this firm, staccato presence: she demanded attention, even when she wasn't speaking. I always liked people like that. Maybe it was because I was quiet, never had much to say, and preferred the noise of other people. The way they'd say anything. I turned to face her and found her watching me. She stared back, patient for a moment. Then she slid over on the curb to get closer.

"I'm Marce," she said.

"Naomi," I said.

She took a hard pull of her cigarette and shook her hair behind her shoulders. Her earrings bounced. Two inchworms dangling on silk.

A bottle crashed on the porch behind us. Marce jumped and twisted to face the noise. A boy laughed and said, "Oh shit shit *shit*."

Marce turned back to face the road and took another hard pull.

"How come you're here?" she said, her voice tight from holding in smoke.

"I knew them in, like, grade school."

"Cool," she exhaled.

The people on the porch had forgotten the glass. They yelled over one another, over the music, arguing about where the homeowners were vacationing. "It's Morocco," they said. "No, it's fucking Cologne."

"I can't believe I'm here," Marce laughed. "That guy was supposed to be my ride. I was at my parents' for the weekend and he said he could drive me downtown."

She was speaking more to herself than me. I didn't mind. Marce was loud but she didn't seem to ask much. Just that I sit there on the curb and smoke.

"What do you do in Toronto?" I asked.

"I'm a server. You?"

"I work at the mall. Here."

I finished my cigarette and crushed it on the ground between my feet. I lit up another.

"Do you like it?"

"No."

"Retail is shit. Do you have a boyfriend?"

"Not anymore," I said. A lie. I'd never had a boyfriend. The kind of blackout sex I'd had up to that point was the kind of thing I'd only remember the next morning when I went to pee and felt this deep muscular ache inside me. I didn't smoke but I liked to drink. I could drink more than every girl in my high school and barely feel a thing. My mother always said we had alcoholics in the family; that kind of thing was in my blood. I should be careful. I never was. I felt bad then, I'd forgotten all about her since Marce stumbled out of the car.

"You know, we might be hiring at my work," Marce said.

"Oh yeah?"

"Do you like nights?"

"Sure."

"Then I might have a proposition for you," Marce said, flicking her cigarette into the road. I passed Marce the pack and she lit up.

"How old are you?"

"Eighteen," I said.

"Tricky," she said. "But not impossible."

I waited for her to explain about the job, but she didn't say anything else. We just sat and smoked. Marce rocked back every now and then to dig one hand into the grass, pulling out dark green clumps. She shaped them into little bird nests, sticking her finger into the middle, making a gentle divot in the green.

"So, are you going to this thing?" Marce pointed back over her shoulder at the house.

"No," I said. I couldn't go home either. All those empty rooms my mother had left behind. I still didn't know what to do.

"Personally, I try not to party much anymore," Marce said. "Whenever I do, I end up crashing someplace weird and full of strangers."

Marce made another nest in the grass.

"I never got good at just going with it. Like when I tried acid and I kept shouting: 'My brain is broken, my brain is broken!' I was never very good at it."

I smiled. Marce laughed.

"Nope, not for me."

She put out her smoke on the curb and wiped her hands on her jeans. She stood up and picked up her purse and shoes.

"I'm going to walk around or something," she said. "Want to wander?"

She held her hand out to me and I took it. Marce seemed to promise so much. Long car rides and long talks and bright rooms in the city. Fresh fruit and tidy refrigerators and somewhere far away from the party behind my mother's empty house and me. Marce smelled like cut grass and had a way out.

"I'll come with you," I said, and Marce pulled me upright away from the curb. I felt dizzy from the smoking and the sitting.

"Cool," Marce said.

She gave my hand a squeeze and let go. Something hot formed in that touch, in my palm, something new and substantial. I felt like I had something important to tell her but I couldn't remember what it was. The world levelled out and Marce tugged me onto the sidewalk, away from the party and into the night.

SKIMMING CRIMSON

Marce let me sleep into the afternoon. She sat on the edge of the bed, wearing a black satin robe embroidered with purple and gold peacocks. She said it made her feel like a geisha or a dancer at the Moulin Rouge. I was just waking up. I sighed and Marce watched a little white cloud rise from my mouth and nose. Marce never turned the heat on. She ran hot.

"Naomi," Marce whined.

She had transcended sleep and hated those lonely night-time hours, the rest I so desperately needed. Marce watched me, my skin tingling almost blue at the edges, like a corpse coming to life. She ran a fingernail up my calf. I shivered and rolled over.

"Why," I groaned.

Marce crossed her legs and the mattress creaked under-neath her.

"Be awake," she said.

"Too much wine."

I pulled the covers up over my head.

Marce lit up a slim and ashed into the cup of water on her bedside table. The cup was pink plastic with a row of daisies printed along the bottom. Marce moved too fast for water. Her mind ran furiously, day and night, skimming the highest peaks of being. She called me for every little thing. We were still sleeping together when we got drunk, and afterward I'd stay up with Marce as long as I could while she paced and smoked and rambled. Theories about the feminine-embodied moon, the land-raping sun. Infinite thoughts smashed together between her ears and dissolved into a fine, buzzing white noise. It felt dangerous, her mind running away, the inside of her skull turning itself out. But on an upward trajectory, that kind of motion felt good to Marce. It felt good to me too. I didn't have to think much when I was around her.

"Pass me my pants," I said.

Marce rented a room with an en suite bathroom. Clothes were scattered across the floor, left where they had fallen in the dark the night before. Takeout containers sat in a tower by the door. She didn't need a kitchen. She got up and went around the room, collecting my things: bra and underwear, jeans and a top. Marce dropped them on the bed and I got dressed under the sheets. I checked my phone.

"You've got work," I said.

"Yeah," she said.

She sat down on the bed and smoked. She chewed a nail, thinking fast about a coffee, about the sidewalk, about keys for work. The church bells up the street erupted, clanging four.

I stopped shifting under the sheets and lay still with the covers pulled up to my chin. My cheeks were flushed from the effort of dressing. I remembered then what I'd told her the night before and how she'd reacted. I'd been stupid drunk and lonely, and I had to get out of there. Marce sensed it too, the quiet tension. She hated that kind of thing – horrible, vacuous silence – so she reached for my hand under the blanket.

"Naoms," Marce said.

I stared at the ceiling. I couldn't look at her.

"Naoms, no big deal, right?"

"No," I said. "No big deal."

Marce flicked ash into the cup.

"Not pissed? Peeved? Perturbed?"

She spoke with a frenzied exhaustion, kind of stuttering.

"No, Marce."

I looked up at her, the hurt formed in miniature, still hiding in the corners of my mouth. I could feel it, but she moved too quickly, leaning over to kiss my cheek.

"Good, great. I'll go to work," she said.

I left while Marce flitted around the apartment, struggling to get dressed. I slammed the door and was gone, but my mind stayed with her. Stayed with her while she turned out her drawers and piled her clothes high in the middle of the room. While she kicked jackets and boots aside and finally settled on a black rayon blend dress and stockings with a red back seam. While she slipped on her sunglasses and left for work, galloping down two flights of stairs to street level.

Marce lived in the market. It got busy on Sundays. Vendors were set up with little tables of leather wallets, cowboy boots, and scarves. Marce fought against a flood of pedestrians, pushing past a bald man biting into a yellow patty, sidestepping a screaming little boy, his face painted orange with black stripes. The ding of a bike bell came down like a hammer on her molars. Marce scurried down an alley. She headed toward the hospital, the high steel walls casting long, cold shadows. A man in a wheelchair and hospital gown smoked and stared up at the dark windows, his head tilted way back so his mouth fell open. His lips were blue at the edges, almost grey.

Marce shivered and broke into a half-run around the back of the hospital. She came up on an intersection and made the last flashing second at the crosswalk before ducking behind a streetcar. The Cleft Hoof was just down the street; a red hoof hung over its door and lit up neon at night. Marce unlocked the door and went inside, met with the familiar smell of a mop soaked in beer, damp wood, and dust. She shut the door hard behind her and left all the lights off. She went behind the bar and poured herself a bourbon, her ears humming from the street.

Marce had the Sunday shift at the Cleft Hoof with Andi. She was generous, and always had something on her, which suited Marce. Coke let Marce talk and talk, totally in time with her brain. It helped keep the big stillness at bay. Andi was always dyeing her hair: red, then purple, then she had settled on blue for a while. Now it was the colour of orange sherbet. Andi and Marce opened the bar and disappeared into the bathroom, locking themselves up in a stall.

"I'm just certain there's a bigger plan for me," Marce said.

"Well, sure," Andi said.

Andi must have been 40. She was from the East Coast and had a kid named Jeb. She always let Marce talk as much as she wanted. She had her phone on top of the metal toilet paper dispenser and she straightened a couple lines on her screen with a credit card. Sometimes the phone would light up with a text, backlighting the coke so the lines looked like thick, fuzzy caterpillars from a fairy tale forest.

Andi did a line and handed Marce her phone. Marce took her turn and her nostrils burned icy hot. Andi set up two more lines.

"I just feel like there has to be something more than this city," Marce said. She could feel the first tingles of chemical euphoria in her jaw. "These fucking lemmings. I saw this thing on YouTube the other day, those rats run in absolute droves over cliffs. Just one after the other, like group suicide. It's insane."

The bathroom door opened and two girls came laughing into the room. Andi popped her head over the stall to check and then nodded to Marce like, *it's okay.* Marce peeked through the crack in the stall door. Two young things. Preening at the mirror and putting on lipstick. They turned on the taps, and Andi and Marce did another line. Marce kept talking, low and fast.

"And I'm like, I'm not like those rats, but people are, you know? They want the right shoes and they kill themselves in rush hour to get to that shitty little desk for those Yeezys. And then they come home and their asshole kids ignore them because they don't even know them, they don't know what those kids want. But fuck if they don't have the best shoes at school. All the other kids have to be jealous of them, that's the best kind of love. It's worth something."

"Fucking Yeezus!" one of the girls said from the sink.

"Hey," Andi growled. She popped her orange head back over the stall.

"Shut the—" she sniffed. "Just shut the fuck up, will you?"

The girls laughed and scrambled out of the bathroom. The door banged shut behind them.

"There's something bigger out there for me," Marce said. "I always wanted to live in the country, on acres and acres, with all these animals. Like birds and broken back ponies that no one can ride but they get to run free in the forest. That's not normal, that's not average. That's not like those fucking people."

"Sure, sure," Andi said. She unlocked the bathroom stall and popped her baggie in her bra. She turned back to check Marce's face and pushed her bangs back off her forehead with one finger. Marce reached one hand up into her dress to check her armpits. She was sweating, all worked up.

"You want bar or floor?" Andi said.

"Floor," Marce said. "I need to move."

"Totally," Andi smiled, snapping her fingers. "Totally, totally."

After work, Marce walked home. The streets were empty. Patient and dark. It was late, or early. Marce didn't know. She walked and she felt her teeth hard, chomping an invisible bit. She should have got some coke for the road from Andi. Marce thought about calling me. We could meet at the Vesta on the corner by my place for a souvlaki and fries. We could set ourselves up at the counter and talk. Marce had ideas. Ideas she needed to bounce off me about this play, a one-woman show about the hyper-digitalization of modern love. Starring, written, and directed by Marce. She felt I would understand. We'd have these love scenes projected in red over her face.

Marce cut back, past the hospital and through the market. She unlocked the main door to her building and took the stairs up. She felt her legs dragging but her head lifted higher still, stretching her neck like an overworked cord, a piece of rope ready to snap.

Marce yanked her door open and dialled my number. The phone rang and rang. Marce peeled off her stockings, shedding them onto the floor. She left the lights off so she wouldn't have to see the bed, the sheets tossed around. She hated an empty bed.

Marce pressed the phone tight up against her face. She stood in front of the window. I didn't answer. I was probably asleep. My voicemail came on and Marce left me a message.

"Be a peach and call me back. I have this thing we need to do. It's a play, I think. And the imagery, it should be twin moons. Both red. Red twin moons, cratered and low in the sky. Maybe that's the metaphor here. People circling each other, gravitational pulls. Maybe we'll project the moons over my face—"

Marce had a cigarette in her hand. She didn't remember putting it there. The cherry smouldered, a tiny beacon in the dark.

"Twin moons," Marce said, exhaling smoke over the bed.

She hated an empty bed. *Where's Naoms?* she thought. In that stillness Marce found herself tracing the day in reverse, back to the afternoon. Me under the sheets. Not pissed? Peeved? Perturbed? No, Marce. The slam of the door when I left. And then back even further, to the night before: my body under her hands, brilliant with elasticity. Marce pulling me forward onto the bed. An ear lobe, tender in her mouth. And me whispering, I love you, I love you, up into the dark. Marce remembered laughing, cruelly, her lips red and sneering. You don't mean it, Naoms. You don't mean it.

The cigarette burned down and Marce's mind slowed. The dust settled. The silence of the room lodged itself deep in her sternum. It stretched, vibrating endlessly through her bones.

"Naomi, I'm sorry," she said into the voicemail. "I don't love you."

She hung up and tossed the phone on the bed. The screen lit up the duvet, the deep folds of the covers, the little depression where I had been that morning. Marce was alone when she felt the shift come, the terrible fall. Like a man jumping out of an office building, his tie caught upward in the wind. It was quiet. She shuddered. Marce hated stillness most of all, where you had to think back to things, remember the way the night went. She'd lost me somehow, or maybe hadn't yet, but would. She had to leave the city, she decided right then. She hugged herself and got into bed. She'd sleep, but she wouldn't stay. She had to keep moving. She decided stillness would kill her before anything else.

SOMEONE TALKS

I got off the train at Union Station and called Marce.

"Let's cook," I said as I passed through the turnstile. "My place?"

"Yeah," Marce said.

I lived in a bachelor on the second floor of a row house. When I got home, I left the front door unlocked and open for Marce. My neighbours hated when I did that. The apartment was stale and grey from my weekend away. I dropped my backpack on the bed and opened all the windows. A warm breeze, one of the last of summer, swept through the room.

"Naoms?" Marce called, just arriving at the front door. "Naoms?"

"Here, up here," I called down.

Marce slammed the door. Her flip-flops slapped up the narrow stairs. The walls in the house were thin. Those old houses were never meant to be split into smaller spaces; the pipes couldn't handle five or six different kitchen sinks. Marce went right for the bed, rolling hastily onto her back. She sighed, a long sigh, and tucked her hands behind her head. Her shirt slid up over her belly revealing the hollow curve of skin between her two hip bones.

I pushed my backpack onto the floor. It had rained all weekend and my clothes were rolled up in a dirty, wet ball. I sat next to Marce on the corner of the bed.

"The weekend was stupid," Marce said. "I'm glad you're back."

"Me too," I said.

She crossed one leg over her knee and jiggled her foot. Her sandal bounced, threatening to fly off, clinging to her toes. Her toenails were painted lime green.

"What did you do?" I asked.

"Dragged Luke away from the Xbox. Got him out on Friday."

Marce uncrossed her legs and lifted her hips off the bed, reaching into her back pocket for a crumpled pack of Vogue cigarettes. She was smoking slims those days. Marce wasn't brand loyal, she wasn't committed to Vogues; she'd buy anything. She pulled out a smoke, pinched it between her thumb and forefinger, and started to roll it back and forth. Then she sat up and kicked off her flip-flops.

"I'm not sure about me and Luke," she said.

It was best to stay non-committal when Marce's relationships took these turns. She got tired of men whenever she moved in with them. In a few months, she'd find their routines boring, their minds dull, the sex languid and uninspired. There was something about folding socks together on the couch that made Marce sick.

"He's just so, I don't know. Indolent."

"Indolent."

"Like, slothful. Like a fucking sloth."

I laughed. Marce grinned and feigned insult.

"I'm serious!"

"I know."

I got up from the bed and stretched. My legs and back were sore. I'd gone home to help my mother with the yard work. Joanne had managed to let the backyard go wild all summer.

"It's really, well, I have gardening gloves and a wheelbarrow," she had said over the phone. "I think it could be fun."

It had rained all weekend. Rain had a tendency to stall Joanne indoors for ages, and she stood at the back door, hands cupped skyward. Indecision was bad for her. It meant crawling into bed and staying there for days.

"It's not so bad out," I'd coaxed.

I'd tried to beat the weeds back. They were taking over the deck, creeping through the slats in the wood. The lawn was hopeless; it hadn't been cut in months, and there's no use trying to mow grass in the rain.

I wondered if the yard was an excuse to get me over, if Joanne had caught the news and seen the weekend forecast. Hoped it might force us indoors together. I'd spent the days in the rain while Joanne fretted at the back door. The sky had cracked with thunder, the downpour rattling down on the deck. It had felt good to be caught in all that sound, thrashing in waist-high weeds. I'd grasped them and pulled, but they slipped through my hands, rooted and defiant.

"Food time?" I asked Marce in the bedroom.

She pulled herself up, still rolling the cigarette in her hand. Marce was a fast, near-manic kind of person but she liked to take her time when it came to consumption. She would swirl glasses of shitty Merlot to check the legs. It took her an hour to eat a crumbly chocolate chip cookie from the bag. She'd dip them in milk and scrape the soggy bits off with her teeth.

Marce followed me into the kitchen. I opened the fridge.

"I think I have stuff for puttanesca," I said.

Marce leaned against the stove. I could feel her familiar nervous energy pulsing close behind me.

"Good, good," Marce said.

I found fresh parsley near the back of the crisper and put it on a chopping board along with garlic cloves, onions, tinned anchovy, fillets, and a big chopping knife. In the overhead cabinets I found tinned tomatoes and black olives. I went to work crushing tomatoes. I didn't like it, the wet feeling and raw insides. I shook my head. They were just tomatoes.

I glanced over her shoulder. Marce was on the counter, swinging her legs and scratching her neck. Hands full, I nodded to the garlic and the cutting board. She jumped down and stepped past me, pressing her hand lightly against the small of my back. I flinched against the pressure of five gentle fingers before she slipped away.

She started to chop. She liked to focus on small, busy tasks. She moved the knife quickly so sharp slices fell in hard, even strokes against the wooden cutting board. It was an old board, beginning to warp from years of use. It had been my mother's. The edges sat unevenly on the countertop, rocking with each slice. For a moment, the only sound was the cutting board and the knife chopping away.

I washed my hands and coated a frying pan in oil. I set it on the element. Medium heat. Marce stopped chopping.

"I'm not sure if it was a good idea for me to move in with Luke," she said.

She placed the cutting board beside the stovetop. The onion and garlic were portioned out neatly into two piles. Marce lifted herself back up to sit on the counter. I scraped the garlic and onion into the pan and stirred them with a wooden spoon.

"I think it was too fast," she said. "He got so drunk on Friday. I couldn't get into bed. He passed out straight across it and I kept yelling over him, hey, hey Luke, hey, but he wouldn't wake up. I literally jumped on the bed."

"That's pretty drunk," I said. I popped the tin of anchovy fillets open and scooped them out into the pan.

"Yeah," Marce said. "Sometimes I'm like, I wish I had a place I could go, like you do with your mom's. Some place where I could go to crash and rest. Anyway, I just don't know. If things go south with him can I stay here a couple days?"

"Of course."

I dumped the tomatoes into the pan and added the olives and parsley. The sauce bubbled up in red lumps. They rose and popped, just air.

We ate beside the open window. Marce wanted to savour the summer air. She twirled forkfuls of spaghetti with light fingers, slurping noodles with pursed lips. We scraped the last of the sauce with the edges of our forks. Marce licked the bowl and lit up.

"Mmm," she said. She took a drag of her slim and sat back. "Want to give me a lift home?"

I pedalled my bike with Marce propped up on the handle-bars. It was downhill the whole way to Luke's place. Marce laughed and laughed. She held on tight. It was dark out and the streets glowed yellow. Light spilled from apartments and houses and shops. We slipped down Luke's street and pulled up to his building. I braked and the bike wobbled. Marce hopped off.

"Thanks, Naomi, you're a peach," she said.

She brushed her lips against my cheek.

Then she was gone, walking up the front stoop, and every-thing was quiet again.

I closed my eyes and could see Marce lying, untouched and waiting on the bed. Her lips moved; her shirt slid up over her stomach. I wondered, not for the first time, why I felt like I needed Marce around so much, if it meant something more than just getting drunk and eating spaghetti. But I knew that if I reached for her, everything would hurt eventually. It was that kind of need. It flared up impulsively when I had too much to drink.

I opened my eyes.

"'Night, Naoms," Marce waved from the porch.

"'Night, Marce."

ELORA

I felt the residual thrill warm in my belly when I opened my eyes. Marce was poised, naked on the edge of the bed, a lit slim in her hand.

"Do you still want to go?" Marce said. She took a drag of her cigarette and looked down at me.

"Yes," I said.

We were supposed to go to Elora. I woke up at Marce's — it was the first time we slept together. The preliminaries to the seduction had been worked out in the early hours at the Cleft Hoof. The last people had stumbled out onto the street and we closed up. We were drunk, as we usually were by the end of a shift, and I was flipping all the chairs upside down on the tables so the legs pointed skyward like stalagmites in a cave. Our eyes met across the room and Marce stalked toward me from behind the bar, slipping her tongue into my ear. It wasn't the first time we'd kissed or even the first time we'd crashed in the same bed, but it was the first time we ended up tangled together, our hands and mouths working busy while some singer cooed softly from Marce's phone, lit up and glowing blue on the bedside table.

We borrowed a car from a regular at the Hoof, a friend of Marce's. We'd been talking about going to see the gorge for weeks. Marce drove, chain-smoking, wearing a cotton halter-top, jean shorts, and a pair of plastic pink-framed sunglasses. It was hot well into the fall that year. The leaves dried out and crumpled into dust. I had on a red cotton baby doll dress, picked from the floor at Marce's. I hiked the hem up so the sun fell warm on my thighs. We put all the windows down and crawled out of the city in wretched traffic. Marce pushed the car through every red light, hot on the tail of the car in front. She gritted her teeth and choked up on the steering wheel. "I hate traffic," she growled.

We got on the highway and sped through rolling farmland, past horses and cows, and we didn't speak. Marce smoked and chewed her lips, her knuckles white.

"Look at that barn," I said.

Marce glanced, eyebrows arching severely over her sunglasses.

At the gorge, we walked the fenced-in trail overlooking the river before Marce decided it was shit, it was a shit view and we should go near the water. We hopped the fence and I followed her down the wooded slope, scrambling behind through trees and bushes and mud. At the river, Marce kicked off her shoes and I did the same. She stepped into the water and started to walk across, the current pulling at her knees. I got in after her, stirring mud and silt into clouds in the green shallows.

I went deeper after Marce. The riverbed was rocky and unstable. The water sucked at the hem of my dress. Marce was in the middle of the river, wading firmly against low white rapids. She held her arms out to balance and drops of water slid from her elbows. Every muscle in her back was tight with concentration. The rapids knocked me and sent me deeper. The cotton dress was heavy with water. I stopped in the middle just as Marce made her way to the other bank. She shook her legs out like a cat. She didn't look back.

I put my head down and slid one bare foot forward, testing the balance of the rocky riverbed, whispering *Please, please, please.* The water tugged at me, threatening cold lungs, heavy arms, and fish picking at my bones. I didn't like going fast. I didn't like river water, or being barefoot, or adventure. *Please, please, please,* I whispered and looked up at Marce. She was perched up on a rock, sunning herself and studying me, her chin cocked up and to the left, waiting to see if I made it to the other side.

I clawed my way through the water, fighting against the current, angry, my eyes fixed on Marce's thick, pink sunglasses.

When I got to the riverbank, I pulled myself up. My legs were trembling. I peeled the dress up over my head and dropped it on the rocky bank. Water rolled down my chest and stomach. I was wearing the same white bra and underwear from the night before. Marce stared at me over her sunglasses.

She got up and jumped from the rock. She stood close to me so our noses were almost touching. I held my breath. Then, she lifted one hand and grazed the skin below my belly button with two fingertips. I shivered and looked away.

Marce laughed. She turned and skipped into the shallows, kicking the water up in a spray. One hundred tiny emeralds broke from the river and flew through the air. She spun around before she could see the brilliant impact, all those ripples in the water.

Marce strolled upstream along the bank. She turned, shielding her eyes against the sun.

"Come on, Naoms," she said.

I picked up the dress and put it back on. Marce was my ride home, my only way out of the gorge. I followed her. The dress clung to my chest; the hem slapped against my legs.

I smelled the river for weeks after that, in my hair, on my skin. I ran the shower hot and scrubbed my skin raw, but it didn't matter. The smell was inside of me, leaking out of my pores.

GHOST LETTING

Before she left me, Marce got really into the supernatural. She drew circles on the floor with salt and left bits of food in her shoes by the door.

"I think I'm being haunted," she told me one night. "I have a ghost."

She was sitting up in my bed. Her pale back hunched over in the dark like a crescent moon.

"Marce, no," I said.

I reached up to run my hand along her spine, but she pulled away from me and looked out the window at the street below.

"I'm sick of this concrete city," she said. "I'm ready for some fucking green."

We'd been like that for a while. Marce knew I loved her, but she couldn't give me what I wanted. I didn't believe in ghosts, but I still tried to play along. I sat cross-legged beside her in the park while she shuffled her tarot deck. She pulled three cards at random and arranged them face down on our pink and yellow gingham blanket. Girls in flip-flops and cropped T-shirts floated across the grass, their arms full of blankets and travel mugs of wine. The last breeze of summer blew them along, hips forward, their bare stomachs tight like sails. Marce revealed our cards slowly, with gravitas: the Ten of Cups, the High Priestess, and the Hanged Man. She sucked a long breath through her teeth. "Fuck," she whispered.

Marce bought an old Toyota Corolla and paid for it with cash. She left me for the mountains. For Vancouver and the ocean. I sat on my bed by the window, listening to the people outside. Children in strollers sang the alphabet, cats fought in the bushes. Lovers stumbled home, their mouths warm with cheap red wine. It seemed like everyone had changed except for me.

SAT. 8:35 PM

Marce, the cats are trying to kill each other again. They kept me up all night, screaming in the bushes. And the fucking students are back on my street. I wish I was in a real neighbourhood, there are so many kids in the Annex. Where are you now? Are you couch surfing? Let me know. I miss you.

Jake hit the six-month sobriety mark after Marce left. He wanted to drive up to Tobermory to mark the occasion. He had quit everything by then – drinking and smoking, pot and porn, everything except chewing his lips and nails. He got skinny and walked around with his chin up, his brow wrinkled.

It was the beginning of the off-season, and Jake got us a deal on a small cottage on the bay. He picked me up in the car, and we lurched north out of the city. I rested my forehead on the passenger side window.

I'd had too much to drink at work the night before. I kept a pint glass by the cash behind the bar. Every time I went to make change, I closed my eyes and drank, trying to undo Marce's arms, her freckled shoulders. Jake picked me up after work and drove me home. When we were stopped at a light, I opened my door and threw up all over Bathurst Street. A bike bell dinged and someone yelled, "Watch out!" A cyclist zipped past. There was a welcome millisecond when the bike blew a cool gust of air into my face just before the tires hit my puddle, spraying puke up onto my shoes and bare shins. I slammed the door and left the window down. Jake pulled over.

"I don't mean to compromise your sobriety," I slurred.

"You're not," he said. "It'll get easier."

With Marce, time often stopped. Moments hovered with incandescent clarity: the curve of her ear, a smoky exhale, her legs pumping higher on a swing in the middle of the night. Everything was paramount; everything had to be preserved in full. I could remember a single wink, distilled down to the micro-movement: the flutter of an eyelash, her tongue running over her left incisor. By the end of our last summer, she was gone but always with me.

Jake got us out of Toronto, out of that aching traffic. We drove west and I peeled my forehead off the window. He drove one-handed, sucked at his free thumb. He'd mutilated himself at a particularly tricky intersection when he bit down hard on a hangnail as the light turned yellow. He'd made his left turn. The skin broke and bled.

SUN. 2:07 PM

Marce, remember when I first moved to the city and we lived with that guy Kenny on Beverley Street? Remember when I sliced my hand open on the fence hopping into the Dunbat pool and you sucked the blood until Kenny got over the fence and gave us his shirt? You were the original teenage vampire, you wore that velvet choker all summer. I thought it would always be like that, you on the other side of my bedroom wall. Call me, okay? I feel like we left on a weird note. I'm fine with everything, really. I just want you to be happy. Maybe we can talk? Or text me and I'll call you, I'll take the charges.

She was reading the messages, somewhere on the road, and I felt connected to her by thin arteries of pavement, yellow veins all matching up and meeting in merge lanes. She didn't answer and I let her be silent. I wouldn't beg. Not yet.

The highway shed lanes. We passed trees, bedrock, and farmhouses. We saw brown cows and horses and a pony with a shaggy white mane. We took the 10 north-west until it turned into the 6 and we started up the Bruce Peninsula. The highway channelled off to a single lane in both directions. The reception on my phone flickered in and out. I didn't hear from Marce, and we didn't stop to pee. Jake was persistent. I was dehydrated.

The highway ended in a fork and a forest rose where the road split. The sky was grey. Jake turned right and we passed a cluster of houses. We could see the water just beyond them, blue and white waves cresting at the end of alleyways and laneways. A copper-coloured retriever bounded alongside us behind a green chain-link fence. We didn't see any people. The sun broke through the clouds, and the water shone crystal green and blue like a billboard for beachside beers. Jake rolled down his window and propped his arm up, letting his thumb dry in the wind, the skin shrivelled and wet. He glanced over at me and grinned, like *Look at me, playing at being cool.* I smiled at him.

We came up on the cottages – five high-peaked roofs nestled in a group at the side of the road. There was a low, clapboard building with a wraparound porch and a sign in the window that read *Bay Cottages Office.*

Jake parked, hopped out and went inside. I stayed in the car.

SUN. 3:43 PM

We got to Tobermory safe. It's a long drive, not that I should be complaining, considering what you're up to.

SUN. 3:45 PM

I think we could be the only people here? There's like clothes lines (I know, small town) and nothing on them.

SUN. 3:46 PM

But why keep them strung up? We haven't seen a single person. It's kind of creepy, actually. If I get murdered, send help!

Jake came out of the office followed by a wiry, tanned woman. He waved for me. I opened the door, set my sneakers down on the gravel with a crunch. The woman sprung toward me, extending one tanned arm for a handshake. I cowered, shy at that small-town familiarity.

"Hi there," she said. "I'm Bridget."

Her grip was soft, gentler than I had braced for. Up close she was small, her shoulders and hips narrow like a teenage boy's. Her face was lined, weathered by the sun. Her lips puckered thin from smoking.

"Hi," I said. "I'm Naomi."

"Nice to meet you," Bridget said. "Okay, Jake, you pull around to number three over there. You can walk over with me, honey."

Jake got back into the car and backed out over the gravel. He steered slowly toward the cottages. I followed Bridget after the car. She walked on her toes, leaning forward in hiking boots.

"Have you been up to Tobermory before?" she asked.

"No, it's our first time," I said.

"I'm up every year," Bridget said. "The season's just ending, so you folks will have lots of privacy. You chose a good time."

A silver number 3 was nailed to the side of our cottage. Marce's voice in my ear, her cards scattered across my bed. *That's lucky. Good equilibrium on three.*

Bridget led us up around the front of the cottage. It had a pine-planked porch and two plastic lawn chairs. Inside were two twin beds, a kitchenette, a couch, a table with four chairs. Linens were stacked on the table. Bridget pointed out the extra towels and showed us the spare blankets in the bathroom closet. She gave Jake a map and two coupons for a boat cruise.

"If you need anything, I'm just in the office," she said.

"Thanks," Jake said.

She smiled and shut the screen door behind her.

Jake and I grabbed our backpacks and cooler from the car. We unloaded a carton of eggs, half a block of cheese, hamburger patties and buns, ketchup, mustard, instant oatmeal, honey packets from a coffee shop, a carton of cream, and two bags of salt and vinegar chips.

I forced a handful of cash on Jake for the groceries. I was worried about money but so was he. We were always worried about money. I'd been saving my tips, though, rolling them up in a cigarette pack at the back of my freezer. When that filled up, I switched my cache to a cereal box under my bed. Marce taught me to do it that way. She had an old-fashioned sense of practicality.

"You pay rent off your paycheque," she always said. "And hang on to your tips." Marce was a good bartender. She got me the job at the Cleft Hoof when I was 18. I grew up in that bar; Marce raised me. She showed me when to be sweet and when to talk back. How to put on lip liner and wear a garter belt. How to find an apartment in two weeks and make sure cabs weren't running the fare over. How to leave bits of food for ghosts at the door so they would stay friendly. "I saw it in a documentary or something," she had explained, breaking saltine crackers up into napkins and stuffing the bundles into our shoes. That was back when the ghosts were still playful, before Marce knew I loved her.

SUN. 4:52 PM

Disregard last message. Alive and well. It's windy here, prob nicer in the summer with the sun out. It kind of looks like a Norwegian fishing island in the sea. The weather changes fast. It's spitting rain outside now. I think we'll go hiking tomorrow or go up to the grotto. There's a map here with all the things to do and we get a coupon with our cottage rental for a boat trip around the coastline to see the shipwrecks. I think we'll do that as well.

Jake went out to the office and bought a bundle of firewood from Bridget to burn in the fire pit, in front of the cottage by the water. He found an old newspaper in the trunk of the car and tore it up. I stayed inside, eyeing him through the screen door. He knelt down beside the pit and blew into the tiny flames, trying to give them some life. He had stacked kindling into a perfect log cabin shape but nothing would catch. It was like he understood what went into making a fire, but he'd never done it before. I opened the door.

"Do you need help?" I called to him.

"No, no, I can do it," he said.

I gave him some distance. The confidence would be good for him. Inside the cottage, time trudged steadily forward as the clouds swirled darkly over the bay. Jake crouched down and blew into the fire pit. Nothing beautiful or brilliant happened without Marce. I found some salt in one of the cabinets. I drew a thin circle around our beds, guarding us against whatever ghosts crept there.

That night we sat beside Jake's fire. He'd dismantled the log cabin in favour of a haphazard pile. He loaded logs on, one after the other. I dragged the lawn chairs off the porch and Jake brought out some extra blankets. The sun set behind the clouds and a cool wind blew off the water, rustling the pussy willows and cattails at the water's edge. Jake made instant coffee with honey and cream. He popped handful after handful of chips into his mouth and chewed steadily. His hands were streaked with soot. I ate the chips one by one, licking the salt from my fingers. I wasn't hungry. Everything tasted like ash.

SUN. 11:14 PM

Marce, do you think we'll forget each other eventually? I keep remembering all these random things, from years ago. Like when we found that eviscerated rat behind work and Andi screamed and wouldn't clean it up so we had to do it with that snow shovel. It was sliced to shit by cats in a tug of war. I can't sleep now because every time I try I see that rat's chewed up head, its missing tail, I can't talk to anyone else about this kind of thing, so I thought I'd let you know. I'm not sure where you are, I hope you're okay. Call me? Or text me and I'll call you. I'll take the charges. Miss you.

In the morning, Jake and I drove around the bay to the lighthouse. We passed Bridget on our way to the car.

The lighthouse was on a long beach. We scrambled over slippery rocks, green with moss. A stick flew out from behind the lighthouse and landed with a splash in the shallows. A dog trotted out and scooped it up in its jaws. It turned and ran back around the lighthouse, trotting toward a couple in the distance. Holding hands in their matching red jackets and black caps, they waved at us, fused together by one long third arm. We waved back.

The lighthouse was small, painted bright white, with red panelled edging. Jake stopped to read the metal placard mounted a few feet away from the red-painted door.

"Lots of shipwrecks here," he said.

"One of those boats takes you to see them," I said.

The only other humans in town faded down the coastline, their dog at their side. Jake stood with his hands in his pockets, his shoulders collapsed forward.

I turned around to look out over the water. The sun reflected white in the shallows. My eyes watered and I squinted. I could see her splashing on Toronto Island, squatting low to pee in the lake, laughing the whole time. I willed myself back to Jake. But there she was, in dark stairwells and bathroom stalls. Running across the park at night, a stolen bottle of Prosecco spraying up from her hands. Backing me up against a wall, giving me what I'd really wanted all along: a kiss on my neck, her hand slithering into my jeans. I shook my head and pressed my hand flat over my wet eyes. Jake reached his hand up for mine. I took it and the sky opened up with rain. We walked slowly over the rocks toward the car.

MON. 12:18 PM

Marce. I don't expect you to write me back. I remember everything with such punching clarity, then I wince from it, who does that? Do you? It hurts every time but I don't want to forget about the summers, when we were at our best. I'm not even sure if it's something I did that made you go, maybe you really just wanted to live somewhere else, somewhere where I happened to not be. Maybe you thought you needed to get away from me.

Jake made cheeseburgers on the barbecue in front of the office. We ate on the porch while it rained. Bridget came over and Jake offered her a coffee. He brought it out to her, piping hot, and we sat on the front steps and watched the water.

"I'd offer you something stronger," Jake said, "but I'm recently sober."

Jake didn't talk about his sobriety; it just existed, somewhere deep within him. The naked earnestness was new on him, and he wore it awkwardly, his hands in his pockets staring at the bay. He was trying the words out, like he'd been rehearsing them on his own. His voice hung level in the air for a beat while Bridget took a long sip of her coffee. At first, I thought she was doing him a kindness, ignoring his vulnerability – a polite oversight. But she sighed and answered, matching his tone.

"No worries, honey. I haven't had a drink in 14 years."

They sat watching the rainy bay, their pasts hanging innocuously above them. Their dark phantoms danced with the same unchangeable reality as the water, the rain, the deep, sunken steel tumours resting beneath the waves. The ships nestled with scarring permanence at the bottom of the bay. The reality of that, truth would not alter: the kicking spray, a hopeless yell, the crash of metal and surge of white foam. It was as it was.

Later in our twin beds, I stayed up listening to the rat-a-tat of rain on the cottage roof. Jake fell asleep fast, his breath steady in the bed beside mine. The wind swept across the porch. The screen door clicked gently on its frame. The air inside was still and clear, untouched by any constant presence. I felt the cavity beside me in the bed, the place where Marce would have been. All I had was the cottage: the towels, stacked high on a shelf in the bathroom, our last drop of cream stowed away in the refrigerator. Jake's keys were on the table, the promise of travel and home defused by the toque and windbreaker on the hook by the door. The door settled on its hinges and the wind died down at last. My eyes closed, falling shut, giving Marce up for a little while.

The next morning was windy but it wasn't raining, so we decided to hike up to the grotto. We took a path along the edge of a lake. The grotto was inside a rock shelf at the edge of the bay. The rock was flat and cool, stretching wide like a prehistoric mouth. It was too cold for swimming, so we hiked up along a ridge to see the grotto from above. I followed Jake up a narrow, rocky trail. We used our hands, propelling ourselves upward on all fours, like wolves. We got to the top, way over the flat rock beach, and I looked down the edge of a sheer cliff and swayed. Jake grabbed my shoulder and pulled me upright. The wind whipped at my cheeks and forehead. Below us, the cave of the grotto opened wide as the water swirled and crashed inside, shooting out back up the edge of the cliff. We listened to the boom of the water echoing off the rock face. We stood still beside each other, watching what time could do, and believed for a little while that we could change. We could make something new.

We drove home the next day, waving goodbye to Bridget as we pulled off the gravel onto the road. We talked the whole time. Jake told me about the time he ran over a bird's egg with his bicycle when he was a kid. How one of the bad kids in his neighbourhood saw him do it, and thought Jake was horrible. While he spoke, he kept both hands on the steering wheel and his fingers out of his mouth.

We pulled off at a small lakeside town for a pit stop. I went to the washroom at a gas station. Jake wanted to find a snack. We drove to the lake and I bought us each a hot dog from a stand. We sat on a green bench and ate them – ketchup and mustard, the way we liked them. I hid the last bite of my bun and hot dog in a napkin in my lap.

"Ready to go?" Jake said.

"In a minute," I said. "I'll meet you at the car."

Jake walked up to the parking lot. I got up from the bench and hurried down to the beach. I got down on my knees and took my phone out of my pocket. There was a red notification over my messages. I was surprised to see it, but it didn't change anything. I'd already made up my mind. I waited for the screen to go black and I dug a little hole in the rocks. I planted the phone and found a flat rock the size of my palm. I pressed it into the screen and it cracked like a tiny rib cage, the hollow chest giving one last breath. The phone shattered under my weight. I lifted the rock away and watched the screen light up white, then blue, then white again before it popped off forever to black nothingness. In the low afternoon light, I felt like I could see it – a hot pink cloud, just for a second, escaping into the air above me. I set the hot dog down on top of the phone and buried it all, sweeping pebbles and stones over the phone's shallow grave. I got up and brushed off my knees and looked down, letting my chin brush my chest.

"Goodbye," I whispered.

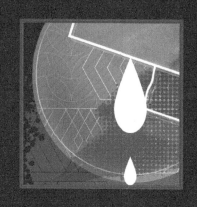

JAKE

SHASTA

It was morning recess and Jake was walking with Shasta on the concrete by the portables. The field was dirty in the winter, all slippery with ice and cold mud. The students were supposed to stay off it. To keep their boots clean.

"I hear the guys are shitting in the locker room," Shasta said.

There had been all these shit accidents announced over the PA system. The principal's voice crackled over the speakers when she said someone had made a poo in the boys' locker room and could everyone please use the toilets. It wasn't an accident though. Jake had walked in on all the guys once, all crowded around Zach while he pushed a long turd out over the blue tiled floor.

"Megan swore it was a little kid," Shasta said. "But I had a feeling it was them."

She tossed her braid over her shoulder. It was long and went all the way down her back. Shasta had hippie parents. They were old, like 50. She wore really baggy pants and sometimes she said *Groovy*, but Jake liked her. In the winter of grade six they walked around the playground at recess and talked.

They passed the portables. Some girls from their class were sitting on the steps. Shasta and Jake went by and the girls started giggling, clapping their hands over their mouths.

"They think we're dating," Shasta said. "But we're just friends."

Shasta was kind. She never made fun of Jake the way the boys in their class did. Nate, Zach, and Chris were loud, and Jake was afraid of the way they jumped off the highest parts of the jungle gym, their jackets unzipped and flapping in the wind. Vultures falling on a carcass.

They picked on Jake about a lot of things, but that winter it was his coat. It was too big, baby blue and puffy with down. It used to belong to Jake's sister.

"I look like a girl," Jake told his mom.

"No, sweetie," she said. "It's unisex. For boys and girls. You'll grow into the sleeves."

Jake knew he would get teased but in secret he liked the blue coat, the way it smelled: of home, clean laundry, and his mom and sister. It made him feel safe. The coat protected Jake out on the playground in the cold. Shasta did too.

Jake and Shasta walked past the girls. Behind the portables, Nate and the guys were pulling a branch down from a tree. They heaved their whole weight against it when the teacher on duty wasn't looking.

"Those guys," Shasta said.

She stomped up to them, her baggy pants caught in the wind around her knees. Shasta cared about injustice a lot. She did presentations on protests in history class. Jake stayed still.

"Stop hurting that tree," Shasta said.

The boys looked up.

"Who's going to stop us?" Nate said.

"Blueberry?" Chris pointed at Jake.

"Suck it," Zach said.

Jake hung back. He tucked his nose into his collar and breathed in the deep home-smell. He felt small.

But Shasta stepped forward, unafraid.

"Everyone knows it's you guys who've been shitting in the locker room," she said.

Her face was red from the cold. Little bits of braid had come undone and were blowing over her face.

"Prove it," Nate said. "You stupid bitch."

The bell rang. The rest of the kids ran toward the portables. Nate waited for Shasta to cry or scream, but instead she rolled her eyes and laughed.

"You're pathetic," she said.

Shasta turned and started to walk away. She looked at Jake and her eyes were still laughing, her whole face red. She looked like she had won a race.

Jake knew he shouldn't have let Shasta stand up for him. He should have told Nate to fuck off, or to eat shit and die. But he just followed after Shasta. A soft blueberry.

"Sometimes the best action is inaction," Shasta said.

They joined their portable line-up and waited for Mr. Carl.

Inside by the coat rack someone jabbed Jake in the back. He turned around and saw it was Nate.

"Your girlfriend's a real cunt," Nate said.

"She's not my girlfriend," Jake said.

"Watch out, Blueberry. After school we're going to get her."

Jake felt sick all day. He avoided Shasta during lunch and afternoon recess. He thought maybe they would leave her alone if he wasn't around. But everyone was talking about her. All the girls were twisting around in their chairs to whisper through cupped hands. They looked back and forth between Shasta and the guys, waiting for something to happen. Shasta sat with her head forward, watching the blackboard. Jake wanted to tell everyone to shut up, but he didn't. They would think Shasta was his girlfriend. He didn't want Nate to kick the shit out of him after school. Jake thought about hard fists, scabbed from fighting, pummelling bloody into his chest.

At the end of the day everyone walked home. They all went in the same direction: out of the school, across the street, and onto the trails. Jake took a long time getting his home-work into his bag, hoping to miss whatever was planned. He hoped Shasta would get away. He hoped she would laugh about it the next day, walking with Jake at recess, those stupid guys. When Jake was the last one there, Mr. Carl said, "Okay, no dawdling."

Jake came up behind the pack of grade sixes on the trail. The trees were winter dead all around them. The boys were bringing up the rear of the group and the girls were ahead of them. Shasta was trailing behind the girls, walking alone. At one point, Shasta looked back and waved Jake forward to come walk with her. He pretended not to see.

The boys moved slowly. Not just Nate, Zach, and Chris. It was almost all the boys in class. They all had their hands in their pockets and stood close together talking before they spread out in a line. Then Nate yelled, "One, two, three!" and the girls scattered and screamed while the boys took rocks out of their pockets and started throwing them.

A rock flew up in a high arc and landed flat against Shasta's head. She cried out. Her mouth flew open and she put her hands up over her head. Rocks landed at her feet, hit her in the legs. They kept coming and coming. Nate looked back at Jake and grinned, like they were in the locker room. Like he was standing over Zach while he shit on the floor. Because Nate knew they had gotten away with it, and Jake let them.

The rocks pounded down on the frozen ground and Shasta kept her hands up. Jake could hear her crying and she started to run away. Zach had the last rock and he took a few steps and launched it at her. The rock landed in a puddle and muddy water splashed up her back.

Shasta disappeared up the path. The girls lingered and waited for the boys to catch up to them on the trail. They were all laughing.

Jake stood behind them, feeling the immensity of his coat, the space in between the fabric and his chest. Jake could still hear the thuds of the rocks hitting Shasta. Could see her last look at him, pleading as he stood with his hands down by his sides. Jake tucked his chin into his coat and took a deep breath. The winter air came in through the stitches and burned cold in his nose.

THE RIGHT COMBINATION

Jake had a bad stomach. A bad immune system, that's what his parents said, anyway. He spent a lot of time doubled over with cramps or dry heaving, so in his senior year he skipped a lot of classes and the office would call and let his parents know. He's got a bad immune system; they'd yell on the phone. Jake's parents were the kind of people that believed in radical self-reliance, in frozen food, and no curfew. School wasn't very important. Jake mostly skipped because of his stomach but sometimes he was smoking pot with Devon on the bike trails between their houses or behind the rec centre. It seemed like a miracle when he graduated but he wanted to go to university, so he made sure to show up for all the big tests and to hand in his papers. In the end, he got off easy. Bs all the way.

The last summer Jake lived at home he pushed his mattress down the stairs and moved his stuff into the basement. He slept better down in the dark. Jake's sister had moved to Australia to be with her boyfriend, and Jake's parents stayed late at work and slept over at their friends' houses or cottages on the weekends. They had lots of friends. In the basement the pipes creaked and the house groaned, swollen from the heat, and it was damp and dark, a good climate for stomach pain and smoking weed. Jake was going to school in Toronto in the fall; not that he had a particular subject he was interested in, but he did have a feeling that moving out might make things different, less frantic, less out of control. More serious. It was easy to sign for student loans, money like that didn't feel real, and university promised something tangible at least, like time spent thinking and reading and sitting up in old, chilly buildings. He thought maybe he'd find something permanent there, something to get excited about, something to start his life with.

One morning he woke up in the basement with his face pressed into the sheets. He caught himself mid-groan, thrashing from the same dream he always had. He said her name as he woke up; it felt hot on his lips. *Devon.*

Jake sat up. He could feel her hair wound smooth in his hand, his fingers tracing her shoulders, her hips. He rubbed his eyes and reached for the bong beside the mattress, broke up some weed, and packed the bowl. He lit up and pulled hard, sucking the flame down into his belly. Pot helped his stomach. He remembered smoking his first joint with Devon before third period in grade nine. They went down to the pit with some other people. It was on the north side of the school, just a ditch behind the football field. Jake coughed and the smoke burned his lungs, turning his insides slow and warm. Jake leaned against Devon's shoulder and someone in the pit asked if they were dating. Devon laughed and helped Jake stand upright. Her palm made familiar, friendly contact with his shoulder. On their way back to class, Jake trailed behind Devon. He watched her ponytail swing back and forth in front of him, the colour of Champagne, then honey, then a red dog running in a perfect green field.

He heard the front door open overhead, the familiar creak of footsteps in the front hall. That's the way his house was, an open-door policy. Kids from the neighbourhood came and went. Jake's parents would tell everyone to help themselves to the fridge and the cupboards, and let anyone crash on the couch whenever they wanted. They were always running out of stuff like milk and eggs and bread. They were always surprised when they did.

The door to the basement opened and Devon yelled down the stairs.

"Jake, are you jerking off? Stop jerking off and get the fuck up here."

The door slammed.

Jake struggled out of bed. He fumbled with the fly on his jeans, wringing his hands so they'd work fast. Sometimes if he took too long, Devon would leave, whistling up the street. Upstairs it was bright. He squinted and paused at the top of the stairs, craning his neck to check back into the kitchen. The house was still. No one was home.

Devon was waiting for him outside by the curb. Jake shuffled toward her, trying not to upset his stomach. The sun burned white in his eyes. He held up his arm to shield his face from the light. It was hot. He regretted his jeans.

"Where have you been?" Devon said.

"Uh, I've been sick. My stomach."

"You didn't answer your phone."

Jake patted his pockets. They were empty. He hadn't used his phone in a while. It was probably tangled up under a pile of clothes on the basement floor.

"Sorry," he said.

"No worries," Devon said.

She was wearing old sweats and a long-sleeved shirt. She had big bags under her eyes, and her hair had been chopped short. It stuck up in uneven clumps. She caught Jake staring at her hair. She grinned and pointed at it.

"You like?" she said.

Devon was thin. Her skin was dry, flaking across her cheekbones and around her mouth.

"It's nice."

"Did it myself."

She faked a curtsy, her fingers pinching the edges of an invisible ball gown.

"Come over. I've got something to show you."

Devon always had something to show him. She would come by the house at night with some reason to roam the streets, draining beers and dropping the empty bottles against the curb. She liked to kick mirrors off parked cars. He knew he'd never be enough for her; he just wasn't made of the same stuff. He wasn't wild, he didn't have any new ideas, but he couldn't help but wonder what it would be like to brush up against her bare skin. To peel her T-shirt off over her head, the fabric catching on the round, full part of her lower lip.

They walked over to Devon's, along the twisting sidewalks, passing lawns gone yellow from the heat. Kids played in the street. They smashed basketballs into the asphalt, yelled into the dry air. Jake's stomach pulsed painfully, each step tugging from his hip. He felt raw in the daylight. Like a bug on the underside of a rock suddenly exposed to the sun. Devon lived with her dad two streets over. They cut through a park. There were some trees and Jake relaxed a bit in the shade. He usually did in dark, damp places. Devon put her hands in her pockets, moving with ease.

Devon's house was set far back from the street, obscured by two old oaks. They crossed the lawn, passed the front door and went along the side of the house to the unlocked mudroom. Devon's dad wasn't home; he worked long hours in the city.

Jake followed Devon upstairs to her room. The bed sat unmade under the windows. The comforter was thrown back and the sheets and pillows had been kicked around into an unsettled, nocturnal nest. The air smelled thick, like cedar. Like Devon.

The curtains were drawn, and the room was dark. Devon's desk sat beside the bed, piled high with books and paper. There was a TV facing the bed beside the door and a blue Nintendo 64 console. Game cartridges were spread across the floor. Jake shoved some aside to make space and sat down.

"You look like shit, you know," Devon said.

"Do you have a joint?" Jake asked.

Devon went to the desk and bent down to open a drawer. Her shirt rode up a bit, showing off her tattoo: a koala bear nestled in the place where her lower back dimpled. Jake looked at his hands, tried not to stare. He'd often catch himself looking at her too long. Her arms and chest. Watching the bend of her collarbone where she broke it playing hockey in grade school.

Devon retrieved a pack of cigarettes. She handed it to Jake. Ten neat pinners were tucked inside next to a red lighter. Jake pulled one out and lit up. Devon took out her phone, her fingers moving quickly over the screen.

Jake smoked and watched her text. There were only a few weeks left in the summer. Devon was set to repeat grade 12, having failed calculus, fitness, and psych. She spent most of her senior year asleep at her desk, stoned from a lunch joint she and Jake split every day. Jake was lucky. Weed never made him that tired.

He got up from the floor and sat beside Devon on the bed. He reached for a ginger ale can on the desk. The top was dusted with cigarette butts. He sucked back the rest of the joint and dropped the roach in the can. It hissed, hitting liquid below. A thin stream of smoke rose out of the can.

"Shawna will be here soon," Devon said, still looking at her phone.

"Shawna?" Jake said.

"She's a year below us. She's coming to hang out."

"Cool."

They sat on the bed and Jake inched closer to Devon. Just a bit, almost imperceptible, so he could breathe in the sharp, wood smell sticking to the sheets, to her skin. He felt his arm brush hers. His skin prickled. Devon kept texting, reached into her pocket and held out a pill bottle.

"Want a benzo?"

She rattled the bottle and tossed it in his lap. The label had been picked away.

"Sure," Jake said.

He cracked the bottle open and shook two flat orange pills into his palm. He popped them into his mouth and crushed them against his molars, dissolving them into a fine powder. Jake swallowed. Devon held out her hand and Jake passed her the bottle. She set her phone down and took two, studying them closely for a second in her palm, before popping them, one at a time, into her mouth. She tilted her head all the way back and swallowed.

"Shawna's bringing blow," Devon said. "This will smooth things over."

She gnashed her teeth and grinned at Jake.

"No tweakers here," she said.

Jake was slow from the joint. It took him a full second to grasp what she'd said.

"You want to do coke today?"

Downstairs, the door to the mudroom opened and slammed.

"Dev," a girl called.

"Up here," Devon shouted.

She leaned forward and rocked her hands, palms up, under her thighs. She sat back and grinned.

There was the rhythmic slap of sandals against feet and then heavy footsteps on the stairs. Jake rubbed his eyes. The pain in his stomach was receding. Pills and weed were mixing nicely, a warm blanket forming over his chest and shoulders.

The footsteps grew louder until a girl was standing at the door.

"Slut," the girl said. "You're lucky my guy was coming through town."

She walked in and kicked off her sandals. She was wearing shorts, the muscles in her bare legs contracting with each movement.

"It worked out okay?" Devon said.

"Oh yeah. He got his ass out here in the end."

She dropped her bag to the floor and sat at Devon's desk, spinning on the office chair to face Jake.

"I'm Shawna," she said.

Her hair was curly and red. Her face, chest and arms were freckled.

"Yeah, I've seen you around," Jake said.

It was a lie. Jake was certain he'd never seen her before. But the words fell, involuntarily, from somewhere high above him. They bounced stupidly out of his open mouth.

"Same," Shawna said.

Her mouth was huge. Pink lips stretched full across her teeth.

Shawna turned back to Devon and the two of them started speaking rapidly. Jake couldn't follow the conversation. He felt the pills trickling down, spreading from his chest to his stomach. The room was moving around him. Shawna waved her arms and Devon laughed. Jake knew his stomach hurt, somewhere, but it was subdued. Soft under fleece. He patted it for good measure.

Shawna spun in the chair toward the desk. Her hands worked on something Jake couldn't see. He felt a small pressure on his knee. Devon's hand. It was almost weightless; her nails were short, bitten down to red skin, each fingertip a silky petal.

"Jake," Devon said.

"Yeah?"

"Bit of benzo, bit of coke?"

"It's the same one," Shawna said. "With that blue shit in it. We'll trip a bit."

Shawna had cleared a space on the desk and opened up Devon's calc textbook to chop. Three fat lines of coke were arranged over pink and green functions, arching parabolic lines. The powder was speckled blue.

The three of them took turns doing lines through a rolled-up five. Shawna went down with a quick snort. Her curls covered her face and brushed the pages of the open book. Devon went next and then Jake followed her, finishing the last line. Shawna rubbed some gummies into her mouth and sucked on her index finger. She opened up Devon's laptop to play music. She stroked the touchpad, leaving a shimmering trail of saliva behind like a slug.

Jake sat on the bed. He felt awake, almost normal. He rubbed his nose and looked around Devon's room like he was seeing it for the first time. The ceiling was high and white. Space opened up forever above them. Jake wanted to let light in so he could see the big room better. He leaned back on the bed and tugged the curtains open, flooding the room with late afternoon orange.

The girls were standing by the desk, choosing music. They looked over at Jake, reclining in the light on the bed.

"What's up?" Devon asked.

Jake put his hand on his stomach. It felt fine. Like it wasn't there at all. Just a big cartoon hole where the ache had once been. He looked at Devon. She was smiling all the way up to her ears. The Cheshire Cat.

"Devon," Jake said.

He sat up and rubbed his hands over his thighs. His fingers lit up, phosphorescent, golden-blue against his jeans. He felt alive. Like Devon had slipped him a hit of acid and he was coming up big-eyed and mellow.

"What, what?" Devon repeated.

Her voice pulled at Jake's chest, grabbing somewhere between his rib cage and throat. He looked up from his hands.

"I love this song," Shawna said.

She took a step up onto the bed beside Jake. The sun was setting behind them and Shawna bounced, her hands over her head, tapping the low part of the ceiling in time to whatever music was coming from the laptop. Her hair vibrated bright red and her legs sliced shadows across the floor. Her flesh rippled in the half-light like a lava lamp, swelling hot.

"Holy shit," Jake said.

Devon laughed. She stood in front of Jake. He wanted her to come closer, to bring her face near his. There was something else starting up in the back of his chest, underneath all that warm energy. An unquestionable confidence, a sharpness of thought he hadn't experienced in a long time. He didn't care about open doors and empty refrigerators anymore. He didn't know why he hid in the basement all summer. Why his stomach hurt, if it ever had. All those nights wasted. He could have kept up. He could have been there, with Devon, watching the day end in golden light. Why was he going to school, leaving her there? Jake knew that if he reached his hands toward hers they would melt together, and their skin would meet at last.

Shawna jumped down from the bed and crossed the room to the door.

"Dev, any beers?" she said and walked out into the hall.

"Garage fridge," Devon said.

She went to sit on the floor across from the bed.

"Feel okay, Jake?"

Jake started to speak but his lips clicked dry over his teeth. He felt his tongue give a little kick. He couldn't string his thoughts together, they buzzed around him, whispers like in a game of telephone.

"I feel good," he managed.

"Of course, you do," Devon laughed.

It was a wild sound. Too loud for the indoors. It pitched high in Jake's ears. He laughed back, *Ha! ha! ha!* forcing it out from his belly so the sounds could layer together in the air.

"Oh man, you are fucked," Devon said.

Shawna came back with three beers. She opened the bottles and passed them to Devon and Jake. They drank. Jake felt his fingers melting watery spots on the cool glass. He kicked back half his beer, trusting his newly absent stomach to handle whatever he put in it.

"Another?" Shawna said, pointing at the desk.

She sat in the chair to chop while Devon and Jake stood next to her. Jake bent down over the calc text and for a second the only sound was the hollow sucking of air and blue powder through the rolled-up bill. Jake stood up and closed his eyes, tilting his head back. He felt the same clarity.

He wanted action. He wanted molten connection to skin. Jake swayed and felt his arm brush up against someone. He opened his eyes and tilted his head back down. Devon was beside him finishing her beer.

"I'll get more," she said. She was gone.

The music on the laptop had stopped. It was quiet. The sun was almost gone, the room glowed with the last day's light.

Shawna set up another couple of lines while Jake finished his beer.

"I'm glad I came over," she said.

Freckles dusted across her nose and cheeks. They were trembling, trying to break free and collide with one another, like planets, like asteroids and supernovas and quasars. How could the entire universe exist on one girl's cheek? He reached out and touched it lightly with his fingertips. Her freckles shivered in response.

Shawna put her hand in Jake's. The hot touch pulled at his arm, moved him out of the room, across the hall and into the guest bedroom. The door closed and everything was dark. They were on the bed. She sucked on his chin, his jaw, his ear. She wrapped her legs around him, digging her knees into the mattress. Jake ran his hands up her shirt and squeezed her back. Her skin was like clay under his fingers. She undid his jeans. Her shorts were gone. When he slid into her, some un-high part of him, way in the back of his brain, surfaced for a second and said, "That's it? That's what this is?" She rocked once, twice, and Jake exploded. He put his face against her neck and his heart beat hard, too fast, and he thought of Devon, alone, maybe outside the door. Three beers in her hands. Looking for him. Something tugged up then, from his balls into his low belly, a sharp pain.

"Fuck," he said.

Shawna rolled off him.

"What?" she said.

He sat up, his hands shaking in the dark. He scrambled for his jeans. Shawna sighed and rolled the covers up all around her like a sleeping bag. She said something but he couldn't hear her. He got up and went into the hall, closing the door behind him.

Jake stood between the two rooms. In the light his skin was yellow, like mould, like decay.

"Jake," Devon said.

She was sitting on her bed in front of him. Her room was dark blue, and the sun had set over the street outside. Her legs were folded up against her chest. She wiggled her socked feet and nodded toward the door behind him. He wanted to tell her he loved her. He knew that was a stupid thing to do. He wanted to beg her forgiveness. He wanted to tell her he'd stay. He wouldn't go away.

"How was that?" she teased, a smile spreading across her face.

She knew where he had been. She just didn't care. Jake swayed on the spot and his stomach kicked up into his throat. He wanted to tell her, but he was going to be sick. He turned and walked down the hall toward the stairs, rubbing his hands on his thighs as he went. They wouldn't hold still. Sensation was building in his fingernails, in the roots of his teeth.

"Jake, just stay," Devon called.

Jake stumbled into the mudroom. A burning pain shot from his hand to his chest. Soon he would be stuck again, unmoving in the dark.

On cue, his stomach lost its ground. Jake opened the door and heaved beer up against the side of the house. His ears popped from the pressure and he couldn't hear anything. He wiped his mouth with the back of his hand. He started for the street. He got to the curb and puked again, all beer and bile. The streetlights were on. The sun was gone, and the sky was dark. His ears popped again, and he could hear Devon and Shawna were laughing, whooping upstairs. He could see them through the bedroom window, two bouncing silhouettes on the bed, music pulsing from the laptop again.

Why did he have to take everything so seriously? Maybe nothing was ever serious. Maybe life was just parties and work and never telling anyone you loved them. Part of him thought, maybe if he went back inside it would be okay. He'd be up there laughing about it too. But then his stomach hurt, and he knew he couldn't. His nose and eyes were running. It mattered to him. It mattered so much he wanted to cry. He wanted closed doors. He wanted to have to knock before entering.

When he got home, before he went down to the basement, he locked the front door. The click of the bolt made him flinch. When he woke up it would almost be time to move out.

SHARING

Jake went over to Caleb and Mara's place almost every night. They lived in an old apartment near the campus on top of an eat-in deli. Their rooms almost always smelled of meat. It turned Jake's stomach. He wasn't a vegetarian; he tried not to think about animal sentience, or whether it was moral to kill and eat living things, but somehow that smell in Caleb and Mara's apartment made the ethics of animal protein difficult to ignore. If it was right, eating meat, then the deli shouldn't have smelled so rich, so heavy, so much like blood and rot and mud mixed together, dripping with fat and set on fire.

One night around 8:00, Jake slouched past the last of the dinner crowd on the restaurant patio, hands shoved in the pockets of his jeans. He let himself into the apartment through the side door. The building was getting old, swelling and listing to the left. The hallway was painted hospital green and lit by flickering fluorescent lights. Jake ducked into the stairwell and went up a narrow, slanted staircase to the second floor.

Caleb and Mara lived in 206. The door was unlocked. Inside it was dark. The blinds were drawn, and Mara was standing in the middle of the living room in a towel. Her hair was wet, and she was trying to untangle it with her fingers.

"Hey," she said.

"Hey," Jake said. He left his shoes on and crossed the room to sit on the couch. He looked at his hands. Mara flipped her hair to the other side and kept running her fingers through it. Wet strands clung to her shoulders and chest.

"Beers in the fridge," she offered.

"Thanks," he said. The apartment was damp, which made the smell worse. Jake wished he could open a window.

"There's this new bar I want to try," Mara said.

"Yeah?"

He eyed the mini-fridge in the kitchenette, pulled himself up from the couch and took two strides over to grab a beer. He twisted the cap off and took a long drink. Then he offered one to Mara.

"Nah, I'm good," she said. "It's called Pharmacy. Have you heard of it?"

Jake took a second beer with him back to the couch. He set it on the floor between his feet and went to work on the first. It was easier to forget about meat with the cool metallic taste in his mouth.

"I don't think so," he said.

"Anyway, maybe we can go after you and Caleb do your thing."

Jake didn't know what she meant, and he was about to say so, but she gave up untangling her hair with a sigh, hiked the towel up to her collarbones and padded barefoot past him, down the hall to the bedroom.

"One sec," she called over her shoulder. "I'll go and get him."

Jake listened closely for the swish of the door, the near-silent click back on its frame. He leaned back into the couch and drank his beer.

He had a feeling Caleb wanted to do an in-person paper turnover. Some of Caleb's customers were green, nervous at the idea of a bought and sold essay. Some of them preferred to get their stuff in hand. Occasionally, they'd get a kid demanding a hard copy so they could type it up themselves. It wasn't very common. The majority of the transactions they did were incredibly lax. Like here's a link to my drive, just drop it in there. Jake preferred lax.

The apartment was dark. Caleb's computer was set up in the corner of the room. He had three big monitors, mostly for gaming. The ceiling was low, brutal, and grey. Everything was neat. Not a trace of dust. Jake still lived in student housing. He'd lucked out every year after his first and skipped the embarrassment of a roommate. In frosh week he got matched with a chatty pothead named Gabe who was studying Classics and seemed truly heartbroken whenever Jake wouldn't go to a party with him. "It will be easier," Gabe would plead, "if we go together."

There was a murmur from the bedroom, the hushed exchange of voices, and a creak from the mattress. The door swished open and Caleb came out into the living room. His hair was damp, and his chest was bare. He had a pair of black socks in his hand.

"How's it going," he asked. He sat down beside Jake.

"Not bad," Jake said.

Caleb bent one skinny leg over the other. He unballed the socks and rolled one on, carefully from the toes up, pulling it high up his calf under his jeans. The bones in his back and shoulders shifted minutely with every thoughtful move.

When he was done, he sat back into the couch, slipped his phone out of his pocket and started scrolling through some messages.

"Ah shit, I need to do something before we go out."

"What's up?" Jake asked. He drained his beer.

"It's complicated. A weird one, if you're up for it."

Jake was always jovial after a first beer. The first beer of the night was easy, it set things in earnest motion. Best of all, drinking fried his sinuses, messed with his sense of smell.

"Then we'll check out wherever Mara wants to go. "

"Good, great," Jake said.

Caleb waited, scrolling on his phone, for Jake to say something else. Caleb always gave Jake the chance to talk. Not that Jake needed the chance. He didn't have anything to say. After a beer, he'd do almost anything Caleb or Mara asked him to.

"This guy's a little hesitant. He doesn't want to do credit, would rather stick to cash."

"Unusual, "Jake said.

"Sure, and I gave him the whole deal, about how I've got a guy who can make it look like a charge from anywhere, the bookstore, Starbucks, whatever the fuck. But still he wouldn't budge so let me see if he's free up on campus and maybe we can swing by real quick."

Caleb pulled up the Hub and tapped the message out on his phone. Jake swapped out his empty beer bottle for the full one at his feet. He cracked it and offered it to Caleb.

"Nah, not for me."

"Which guy is this?" Jake asked.

"1BASTERD."

Jake nodded and drank. He found Caleb customers on the school's file sharing system, the Hub. It was a relic. Students in the early 2000s set it up to upload and download music, porn, and movies. It wasn't mainstream anymore, and after the streaming boom the Hub had taken on a sort of darknet vibe. For instance, its chat feature was the fastest way to get connected anonymously to mail-order pot, and the content lineup featured mostly snuff videos of questionable legitimacy. It was a well-known source for services, like Caleb's papers-for-purchase.

Jake was Caleb's front of house staff. He chatted up kids like 1BASTERD with one of his rotating usernames: WILDPUG, GREINWORK, or MASSTERCROFT. Caleb mostly sold to first years. Jake never asked where the papers came from, though he suspected Caleb did a lot of the polishing himself. He had a certain pride about his product.

Mara came out of the bedroom. She was dressed in a white T-shirt and black jeans. Her hair was twisted up, tangled and wet on top of her head. She tossed a shirt at Caleb.

"Shall we?" she said.

Jake felt the second bottle already empty in his hand. He set it down with the other on the floor. His stomach felt hard, full of liquid. He hadn't had dinner. Mara and Caleb never seemed to get hungry.

Caleb pulled his shirt on over his head and got up. A white T-shirt and black jeans. They matched perfectly. They never wore jewellery and they hated tattoos. Mara bent to pick up the empty bottles from the floor and Jake jumped up to help.

"I got it," she said. She took the bottles to the sink to rinse them out. Jake swayed, dizzy from getting up too fast. Mara set the bottles on the counter. They stood out, intrusive in the bare apartment. There were always beers in the fridge, but Mara and Caleb weren't drinkers. They kept them in the apartment for Jake.

Caleb got up and stretched.

"Okay, go time," he said.

Caleb went back into the bedroom and came out with a brown paper envelope.

"Old school," he said, handing it to Jake.

Mara locked the apartment and they stomped down the stairs, into the underground garage. They piled into Caleb's car and headed up and out to the fading daylight. Jake put the brown paper envelope onto the empty seat next to him. Caleb rolled all the windows down. Jake was feeling slightly buzzed; his legs were gooey underneath him in the back seat.

"We're meeting this guy at the Earth Sci building," Caleb said.

The sun was just sinking over the buildings behind them. The open windows caught a breeze. It tugged at their shirt-sleeves and blew golden over their skin. Mara opened the glove compartment, looked inside and then closed it. She turned around to face Jake.

"I think there's a mickey somewhere back there, if you want anything. Maybe it rolled under?"

Jake leaned forward and fished under Mara's seat for the plastic bottle of vodka. He cracked the cap and took a sip, burning his lips, throat, and chest so they felt like sunlight. He took a swig and tapped Mara's shoulder, gesturing toward her with the bottle.

"I'm okay," she said, wrinkling her nose. "Vodka is too much for me."

"Okay," Jake said.

He sat back and drank. Caleb pulled up beside a streetcar at a red light and then turned left into the southwest quarter of campus. He parked down the street from the Earth Sci building, a building made almost entirely of glass with trees and a garden growing up on the roof. It stood out in the quarter surrounded by Sixties brutalism. The Arts Faculty loomed across the street, hulking and flat with narrow slats for windows. Students dotted the street and stood around doorways smoking.

Mara let her arm dangle out the window. The sun was low. Jake poured another dose of vodka down his throat. He swallowed hard and felt the telltale tug, sharp at his jaw, and nearly gagged but his stomach took the vodka and held steady. He was grateful all the windows were down.

They waited for a few minutes while Caleb texted on his phone. Mara hummed and started to rotate her hand in small circles. Jake felt nervous around them when things fell quiet like that. They didn't have much to say to each other. Mara was in the same year as Jake, but he'd never have met her if not through Caleb, and the only way they would have met was through the Hub. It seemed tenuous, at best, the stuff of coincidence. People like Mara and Caleb slept all day and only went out at night when the sun was setting. They were beautiful and thin and always seemed to have cash. They never got hung-over. They were different from Jake.

"I think that's him," Caleb said.

He nodded up the street. Jake ducked his head and looked up so he could see out the windshield. Mara didn't turn to look. She just kept humming and twisting her hand.

A guy in a hoodie was coming down the street. He was tall and stooped. He had his hands in his pockets and he was looking conspicuously back and forth. The bottoms of his pants were sloppy and torn at the hem. His left shoe was untied, and the laces kicked up and danced with each lumbering step. It must have been 1BASTERD. Caleb's customers had a very specific look. They were always guys – computer kids, gamers, and basement nerds. Jake remembered his own first year at school, grabbing yesterday's socks off the floor and stumbling late to lecture.

Caleb leaned forward and curled his hands around the wheel.

"All set, Jake?"

"Yeah," Jake said.

He swept the envelope off the seat behind him and got out of the car. He walked quickly up the sidewalk to intercept 1BASTERD. The sun was low, and the street was cast in long, cool shadows. 1BASTERD hadn't noticed Jake heading toward him yet. He had wide shoulders and a round middle.

Jake checked back at the car. He could see the outline of Caleb behind the wheel, Mara in the passenger seat, her hand still hanging out the window.

"Hey," a voice said.

Jake turned back around. 1BASTERD was right in front of him.

"Hey," Jake said, startled. He was slow from the vodka and beer. 1BASTERD was tall, massive really. Jake ran his hand through his hair.

The guy nodded at the envelope in Jake's hand.

"You're the...?"

"Yes."

"Right."

Jake was glad that he was a bit drunk. 1BASTERD stared at him, blank and helpless, his mouth slightly open, but he was imposing by sheer stature. Like a gentle bear. He could swat Jake away with one hand if he wanted to.

"Let's find a place to sit," Jake said and pointed at the front of the Earth Sci building to a row of benches. He needed a place to count out cash. There were a few students passing every now and then, but night classes were in and there wouldn't be any crowds until just after 9:00. Jake started for the benches and 1BASTERD trailed behind him. Jake sat down at one end and 1BASTERD sat at the other. His knees were huge, nearly twice the size of Jake's.

"Okay, so, you're here for the paper?"

"Yes."

Jake worried that he was taking too long. He didn't like to make them wait. He checked back down the street, but Caleb was still there. Mara's hand was gone, back inside the car. They were two black shadows, watching him.

"It's two-fifty?"

"Yeah, two-fifty."

1BASTERD pulled some bills out of his hoodie pocket and handed them to Jake, who did a quick count with the envelope on his lap. Satisfied, he passed 1BASTERD the paper.

"Okay, that's it?" 1BASTERD said.

"That's it."

Jake got up and 1BASTERD nodded. He stood and folded the envelope in half, jamming it inside his hoodie. Jake cringed at the sound of paper crumpling.

"Do you write the papers?" 1BASTERD asked.

"No," Jake said.

"Right. Well, bye."

"Bye."

1BASTERD started walking north, back to the end of campus with all the student housing and dorms, back where Jake lived. A bad feeling came over Jake as 1BASTERD walked away. The slow walk, his messy laces and belly. Jake got sad, then, sad at the way the kid looked walking away. Why didn't he just write the paper himself? Jake tried to shake the feeling off, but he was drunk, and it was too late. He had a habit of getting too drunk, too fast, too early. He was prone to moodiness, a sort of melancholic indulgence, like when he thought too long about slaughterhouses and pigs crammed onto trucks. He got up from the bench and hurried back to the car. Caleb smiled out the open driver's side window.

"What a kid, right?"

"A mess," Mara laughed. "Bet you need a drink after that."

Mara slid her hand over onto Caleb's thigh and a violent little hate, the shape and size of a spider, flared up inside of Jake.

He opened the back-seat door, bent inside and grabbed the vodka. He slammed the door before he knew what he was doing. He tossed the bills through the open front window at Caleb. 1BASTERD had paid in fifties.

"What's up?" Caleb smiled. The bills fluttered and fell to his lap. He didn't pick them up. Two hundred and fifty dollars. He didn't need it.

Jake turned and walked back across the street. His head swam, cloudy. The sky was dark. The sun was gone.

"What the fuck was that?" Caleb laughed. Jake shoved the mickey into his back pocket and hurried up the sidewalk. He heard the car pull away, felt the headlights beat across his back as Caleb and Mara sped past him, pulling a sharp left at the stop sign ahead.

He knew he was being strange. Unpredictable and odd. He got like that sometimes. He had a feeling he was supposed to be the butt of some joke from the start of the night, that they knew, as soon as he got to the apartment, that he couldn't say no to beers or doing the paper turnover. He never did. Mara and Caleb used to stay up all night laughing at Jake while he got drunk and goofed off. He'd pass out on their couch and wake up with that smell of meat all around him. He'd be sick right out on the street, beside the deli patio where people were having their mimosas, blintzes, and bagels with lox. Jake wasn't a man of action. He was only good at showing up.

Jake took the mickey out of his pocket and drank hard and long. The vodka roared through him. He caught up with 1BASTERD, just a few steps ahead of him on the sidewalk.

"Hey," Jake called.

1BASTERD turned around. Jake shoved the mickey back into his pocket. He felt strange, like his chest was swollen with good news. Like when you were a kid and you woke up with a secret leftover from the night before.

"It's Caleb DeFriest," Jake said.

"What?"

"Caleb DeFriest, fourth-year computer sciences," Jake said.

1BASTERD stared at Jake.

"Okay," he said.

"In case you're not happy with your grade. Or whatever."

Jake could feel his chest heaving from the effort of it. The betrayal, the secret set in motion.

"Oh right. Thanks." 1BASTERD nodded and stepped back before giving Jake a slight wave. Then he kept walking. Jake stayed put, his hands in fists, and watched.

The doors to the Earth Sci building and the Arts faculty opened and students poured out onto the street. There was sound everywhere, all at once: voices bubbling over, laughter. Girls in groups walked with their backpacks, thumbs hooked in their shoulder straps. Jake stayed still on the sidewalk and let them sidestep him. "*What the fuck?*" they said as they passed. He cared but didn't. He felt like he was sitting in the middle of some fast moving water. Like he'd set a stone in the middle of a river and changed the current forever. He wanted to go back to the start of the night. He would have done it differently. But he couldn't then, so he carried himself back to his single room. He finished the bottle on the way home, and for a little while he didn't have to worry about what he'd told 1BASTERD. And when he finally fell asleep, he couldn't taste or smell or see anything anymore.

OLD PLUMS

Marce was behind the bar yelling.

"You had too much. Jake, you idiot. Time to go."

Marce never gave Jake the boot so he knew it was bad. He couldn't find his jacket. She was dragging him out by the back of his shirt. He said something wrong, he knew it, but he couldn't remember what.

He'd been sitting with that freckled girl and her friends in the corner of the bar. They came up to Jake when he was drinking alone and said, "Hey, come sit with us, come meet Miranda." So he did and they ordered shots. Marce poured whiskies at the bar and one of the other bartenders, the girl named Andi with the blue hair, brought them on a black tray. Jake put cash on the table. He'd won big on Replay Poker, doubled his rent that afternoon by taking this guy BIGPIG all in.

Jake was outside on the street and Marce was gone. His jacket was draped over his shoulders. He wasn't sure how that happened. It was cold out, he knew, but he couldn't feel it, so he left his jacket the way it was and started yelling, "This is Canada, fuck you, fuck you." A guy with a buzzcut and a shiny leather jacket bumped him on the sidewalk. The leather was black with a thousand buckles. As the guy collided with Jake and pushed past him, Jake felt the buckles scuttle over his skin. He shivered.

The bartender with the blue hair came outside. She cupped her phone up to Jake's face so he could see the lines of coke, white and glowing on the screen. That straightened the world out a bit, and when he looked up the street snapped sharply into focus before going soft again like an optometrist's lens flicking over his eyes. One or two?

The bar sign hung over them, a neon red hoof, and there were faces lit up by candles inside the front window, all orange and black mush. The girl with the blue hair sent Jake off with a wave, *bye*, and her face was mush too.

Jake turned and started off down the street, his cape flapping behind him. He thought maybe he said something about jamming one of those girls in the back room. Maybe that's why Marce kicked him out, maybe they told her. He wanted to sleep with them, in a wistful sort of way, like, oh, wouldn't it be nice to rub our ultra-sensitive, fleshy parts together? You know, Down There? But it probably didn't come out that way. It probably came out like let's jam in the back room, and then he would have reached for them. He was never sure why he did that, tried to grab like a kid at a bag of candy, but he did, and they hated it. They were right to hate it.

Talking to women never worked out for Jake, especially if it was in bars. If Jake was in a bar, he was drunk. And not a contained, coy drunk; he couldn't be like that anymore. He was a wreck. He saw other guys do it from across the room. With a look. And sometimes they got there. Jake had seen it happen. It was a numbers game, maybe. Like, look hungry at enough girls and one will be hungry back. He shouldn't have used the word *jamming*, probably.

Marce caught up with him, out of breath. She'd chased him down the sidewalk.

"You need a cab," she said.

She was trying to hail one. Marce had broad, thin shoulders. She could have filled out with muscle easy. She could have been an athlete. Maybe she was once. Volleyball or swimming.

There was a yell from across the street. People pointing at Jake and laughing. Mushy blobs. He swung at them.

"You cunts! You fucks!"

"Jake!" Marce pulled him back from the street. Her face was set, serious.

"Oh, why Marce? Why're you so…?"

"Let's go."

Jake was having a hard time with his hands. Marce reached for him and he threw a sloppy punch, batting her arm away. Marce stepped back.

"I'll jam them up, I'll—"

"Goodnight, you fuck," Marce said.

Jake was alone.

In another bar, Jake felt his cape slip from his shoulders onto the floor. There was brown liquor in a sturdy glass and an old man on the stool next to him. The man didn't have a drink. He didn't have any teeth. He smelled sharp, like piss. He sat close to Jake and said, "I'm a good person. I'll behave myself."

"You're a good person," Jake said.

"I'll behave myself."

"Good."

❖

In the morning, Jake was older.

He spat into the toilet and he felt nothing. The sink was clogged with puke, bright pink and foamy like Champagne sea foam.

It was morning but it was dark. The curtains were open, and the sky was just turning from black to blue. There were two girls on the floor sitting cross-legged in front of the computer. One was wearing a shiny purple dress. The other was in one of Jake's old T-shirts. Her legs were bare, folded underneath her. Like story time in kindergarten.

They looked up at Jake. He couldn't smell anything.

On the counter in the kitchenette sat an overstuffed ashtray, a pack of rolling papers, and a grinder. Tinfoil crumpled and burned with a lighter.

There was a newspaper spread out on the floor between the girls and a pile of dark purple plums.

"Fruit?" one girl said.

She was holding a knife. Slipped it into the plum skin. It passed through cleanly, tracing a wedge out. She plucked it away from the pit and held it up to Jake.

He took it and bit into the fruit. He couldn't taste anything. Driblets of juice trickled down his chin, onto his bare chest.

The girls were high. Their pupils were wide, placid in the half-light. They sniffed and smiled. Their faces peeled back, their foreheads wrinkled deep. Two pink mouths stretched back into gummy grins. One of them had braces. Their lips were wet. One started to sing.

"Jakey, Jakey, Jake. Cut your throat with a garden rake."

Jake stepped back. He wiped his chin with the back of his hand. He was afraid of the knife and the song. He was afraid of the burned tinfoil on the counter. In the morning he was older, and he wanted the girls to leave.

"Get out," he said.

They laughed.

Jake went into his room. He closed the door and sat down with his back against it. He heard the girls gathering their things, packing up the plums. His heart pinched weakly and fluttered in his chest, struggling against the night before. Trying to keep Jake alive. The girls opened the front door and left, slamming it heavy behind them. A bird chirped outside. The sun was rising. Jake rubbed his chest with a fist and went to his computer. BIGPIG was online. Jake entered $500 in a game and won. He was dizzy. BIGPIG was always a sucker.

Jake decided to go down to the Hoof. Just to leave Marce a tip. A big tip. She tried to get him into a cab. Jake leaned back in the computer chair and watched the sky grow big with light. A streetcar rang its bell down below. He would try to sit quietly at the bar and have one beer. Just one to smooth him over. Then he'd leave Marce the money and go back home. He would, this time.

AT THE BOTTOM

Jake was coming out of the garage side door when it swung in on him and smashed into his face. He started to bleed straight away, and his vision went white as he stumbled back onto the concrete and fell on his ass. He didn't see it coming, being on the other side of the door, but he'd also spent the afternoon drinking. Double rum and Cokes with two twists of lime. He wasn't particular but when he got drunk he liked pretending to be. He'd smoked a joint in the car on the way home to level out, a sophisticated sative hydroponic called Meth, and his nose was gushing hot through his fingers. He knew he was hurt, but he couldn't feel anything. Not as much as he was aware something excruciating was happening and he felt very satisfied it was happening.

He wanted to see it, so he pulled his hands away from his face. His vision started to dissolve at the edges, and he looked at the garage floor.

Yes, there was blood. A red puddle on his lap, on the floor between his knees. He tried to get up but stumbled back again.

"Well, Magoo, you've done it again," Jake said.

It came out as a cough and a gurgle. Everything was sticky with blood. He tested his front teeth with his tongue. One clicked forward, a millimetre, barely perceptible, but loose, and pain like ice shuddered up the root into his palate and split his head in half.

"Oh my God, I'm sorry," the voice said. "I – do you need an ambulance?"

Jake mashed one hand over his face to see what it felt like. His nose was crushed, and everything was wet down to his chin. His hands were covered in blood and snot and these stringy black chunks that looked like worms or pieces of brain. His stomach lurched. The white started to creep in again.

"Whoa, easy."

There was a hand on his shoulder.

Jake looked up past his hands. There was a pair of feet. Blue sneakers with white laces. They were too clean for that garage, for the puddle on the floor. The hole where his nose had been started to throb with pain that made him dizzy. Or was that the Methistopheles? He'd forgotten he was high.

"Let me call," the voice said. The hand let go of his shoulder and the shoes started to pace back and forth.

"Yes, hello? I think I need an ambulance."

Jake didn't want an ambulance. He tried to get up again but puked instead.

"I think he's in shock."

Jake felt for the car keys in his pocket. How had he gotten in the garage? He couldn't remember. He'd been driving with the window down, smoking the joint. Then his face met the door.

"Okay, thank you. No, I'll stay with him."

The shoes stepped back toward Jake.

"Is there someone I can call?"

"No," Jake gurgled.

Jake didn't have anyone anymore. His friends moved to Thailand and left Jake their apartment. Their car too. He was supposed to take care of everything until they got back. The truth was Jake knew they weren't coming back. That was the point of leaving. Jake could have said to call his mother, but he didn't actually have her phone number anymore. Why was it that some families spoke and others drifted into silence? What was that? At the dinner table when he grew up, no one talked; the only sound they made was chewing. Were they supposed to have something to say to each other? Something to talk about on the phone?

"Hey," the voice said.

It occurred to him then that the voice belonged to a girl. She had done the door swinging. It occurred to Jake that she'd been down there in the garage with him for too long already. He was probably holding her up.

"Sorry," he slurred.

He got up. His head exploded. Blood dripped metallic down his throat. Jake spat between his feet, foamy and pink on the ground. He kept his head down, away from the girl. The world seemed to tilt forward and Jake shivered.

"Rock bottom," he said.

"What?"

The hand touched down on his shoulder again. This time Jake turned his head to look at it. It had perfect nails. Healthy. Clean cuticles. White-tipped and long. Jake looked up at the girl. She was small, normal. High cheekbones and bright, grey eyes. There was an elegant asymmetry in her face – her nose turned up slightly to the right and her mouth curled under at one side, almost comically serious with concern. She had a yellow backpack slung over one shoulder. She was probably a student; there were lots of students in his building. He stayed away from them. He'd withdrawn in his last semester and cut his losses. On campus there was this cluttered frivolity he felt disconnected from, a wildness of thought. He wasn't political or interested or keen. He wasn't anything.

"Are you okay?" the girl asked. "You need some air?"

She took her time getting Jake out of the garage, helped him walk up the stairs while he stumbled, stinking of pot and beer and blood. He couldn't believe he'd gotten the car into the garage. A miracle. He looked at the girl's ass once on the stairs and then looked away. He felt like a dirty old man.

It was sunny outside and cool. Jake sat on the sidewalk outside the building. The girl got down on her knees in front of him. People were out shopping or walking their dogs. They had their earbuds in, their music cranked high. They side-stepped Jake and the girl without missing a beat.

"Are you okay?" the girl said.

Jake nodded.

"Have you been drinking? Smoking?"

Jake looked up at her, holding his temples. The blood ran out of his nose freely, over his chin and onto his pants. He didn't care. He looked up at her, let her see him, sweaty and wasted out in the sunshine, and he didn't care if she knew.

"Yes."

She nodded, and it seemed for a second, as if she understood, as if she accepted him. If she stayed, he wouldn't have to lie or pretend. She already knew.

"I have a thing about that," Jake said.

"Oh."

"Drinking too much."

Jake tilted his chin up toward the grey brick building. The sun bounced off his window on the second floor. He didn't want to go up there. Back into the dark alone. He closed his eyes and heard the sounds of sirens far off in the city. Maybe she would get into the ambulance with him. Maybe she would stroke his forehead and push the dirty hair away and tell him everything was going to be okay. Maybe she would take him home from the hospital and make sure he took his meds and stay and keep him safe for a while.

Jake opened his eyes and felt himself reaching for her, flailing in daylight for her hand. The sirens were louder, closer now. She stood up.

"You should tell the paramedics," she said. "Alcohol and pot can thin out your blood, make it harder for it to clot and stop the bleeding."

She looked out over the street and stepped back.

"They'll be here soon, I'm sorry but I've got to go."

She hiked her backpack up higher. It was big. Heavy with books. Probably biology and physics. Maybe she wanted to be a doctor. Maybe that's why she kept her hands so clean.

"You seem okay. You're okay, right?"

Jake looked down and spat.

"Okay, I'm sorry," she said again.

She turned and walked away down the sidewalk. The ambulance came down the street, sirens blaring. It pulled up across from the building and the paramedics pointed at Jake.

Once they saw him, they seemed to slow down. They took their time getting the stretcher out of the back. Jake stayed where he was. He wanted them to scrape him up off the sidewalk. He wasn't an emergency.

BURN SLOW AND CATCH FIRE

In the winter, Jake got desperate. He practically begged girls to sleep with him and threw veritable tantrums on the street when no one looked at him twice. He got older all of a sudden, and a bit fat, which killed any shot he ever had at sexual aloofness, at being a cool guy. Drinking wasn't fun anymore and going out was a total chore. By the end of most nights, Jake found himself back home, drunk, with a game of Texas Holdem on the screen. He spent a lot of time online, ordering acid from Japan or paying for live cam action with real-looking girls, suckered in by the promise of a gap-toothed smile, an authentic southern drawl, and that's about the time he happened upon Kevin in the White Room.

It was another kind of live cam thing. Not a girl, just a stream of this guy in a windowless, white room with a clock running on the page. Kevin was the sole subject for an experiment that was testing spontaneous human combustion in a controlled setting. The experiment seemed to consist entirely of sticking the guy in an underground bunker and filming him 24/7 to see if he randomly exploded.

The White Room had a low ceiling and the walls and furniture were all white. There was a desk, a chair, a bed, and a wide, stainless steel entry door that never opened. There were at least 12 cameras set up and the stream would cut between them depending on what Kevin was doing. There was a high angle of the whole room, a medium shot framing the bed dead centre and a confessional cam mounted on the wall over the desk. Kevin did confessionals a lot, like, "I'm still here in this fucking room, still waiting to combust. My meals are regulated to ensure some reasonable parameters. I'm sick of chicken salad," and so on. It could all have been pre-recorded, but as far as Jake could tell there were months of unique footage. That in itself was pretty impressive, pretty rare – just a guy sitting in a chair doing push-ups or jacking off or reading a book. It was that boring. It could have been real.

Jake watched Kevin a lot, and there seemed to be some understanding that Kevin would eventually burst into flame. For one, Kevin spoke into the confessional cam like a dying man. He talked about being a bully when he was a kid; about not knowing how to put on a condom the first time he had sex. He talked about the outside world as if it didn't exist for him anymore, as if he had to settle his life's transgressions and confess them to the internet.

Kevin would look up into the camera and say something like, "I've eaten so many sandwiches down here, when I explode everything will be coated in chicken salad, innards, and mayonnaise." When he talked like that, Jake felt a dark part of him open up. It was the same feeling he got when he had his first drink of the day.

Jake didn't see many people anymore. He spent his days in his apartment and went out to the Cleft Hoof at night. It was his favourite bar, a long room sandwiched between a pharmacy and a 24-hour laundromat. The Hoof filled up fast every night of the week. It was a small, hot space with square wooden tables and a bar running along the back corner. Jake liked to sit and drink and pretend he was meeting someone in the middle of all that noise.

His sort-of friend Marce worked there behind the bar. She was tall, redheaded, and manic. She'd throw him a free beer every now and then. Marce was sleeping with another girl who worked at the bar, Naomi, and they were pretending no one around them knew. Naomi was quiet, and Jake felt, sometimes, that she confided in him with looks. Naomi would pour drinks and glance darkly over his shoulder at Marce, who liked to chat-up customers just a bit too long and let her fingers rest on their shoulders before she slipped to the next table. Naomi would grab a bottle of whiskey by the neck and pour Jake a shot. Her eyes fixed firmly on Marce; her jaw clenched tight.

One night that winter, Naomi was distracted with Marce and she lost track of Jake's drinks. She usually watched his intake closely, cutting him off after four or five rounds of Jameson and beer, but that night he got pretty wasted.

After last call Naomi set a glass of water down in front of him, like she always did, and Jake didn't want to be drunk anymore. He wanted to peel back his skin and spill his guts loose on the ground. He got up and started grabbing tea lights off tables and smashing them against the floor and the walls. Someone screamed and Jake started to laugh. He was such an idiot for getting hammered in the first place. A candle hit the wall and Marce screamed again, pushing Jake out the door. He forgot his credit card at the bar.

In the morning, Naomi texted Jake. She was swinging by to drop his card off. She probably got his address from Marce.

He wished she wouldn't come. He lost cards all the time, left a steady trail of consumer debt wherever he went.

Jake drank two beers fast. He felt the blood pumping way up into his head. It pulsed hard between his ears, trying to repair all those broken connections, those vital neural cells he had destroyed the night before. The buzzer went off and Jake let Naomi up. She knocked twice hard on the door and Jake said, "It's open." She came inside.

Jake was waiting for her on the couch. He was wearing his indoor clothes. Jeans and a fleece sweatshirt. Outside he liked to wear button-down dress shirts tucked into grey pants. He liked to dress like he had somewhere to go. Like he had loosened his tie after a tough day and tossed it in the back of the car.

Naomi's nose was red from the cold. She had an open face with a practiced neutral expression. Her eyes were dark brown, almost black. She crossed the room and handed Jake his credit card. She turned her eyes over the apartment, taking it all in, the bare walls and the three computer monitors set up in the corner. Jake tried to guess what she might be thinking. Like, Wow, what a loser, what a recluse, what a drunk. It stinks like hangover sweat and tomato soup in here.

"What are you watching?" she asked.

Two of the monitors were off and the other was streaming Kevin in the White Room. Jake left Kevin on all the time. It was like having a roommate without the mess or the condescending tone when Jake cracked his first beer before noon.

Kevin was sitting on his bed listening to an old iPod with a crank wheel and no Wi-Fi. He had one leg crossed over the other and bounced his foot in time to the music. He flipped through a copy of *Thrasher*. He said he used to skateboard, that he loved the sound of grinding concrete. He was slight, had the right build for it, and he often paced the White Room with this cultivated slouch meant to secure his frame low to a board.

Naomi and Jake watched Kevin, Jake from the couch and Naomi from the middle of the room. She still had her jacket on and her mittens in one hand. She had a dark green scarf wound high around her neck.

And then the big stainless steel door opened. The view changed and cut to a high corner camera, a full angled shot of the room, and a person wearing all black came through the door.

Jake got up from the couch to get a closer look. The person in black was carrying a red cafeteria tray with food on it. A white bread sandwich, a carton of milk, an apple, and a granola bar. The kind of food you might see kids eating in the movies. The door closed behind the person in black and the camera cut in to show a black hoodie, balaclava, gloves, and shoes.

Jake sat down in the computer chair while Naomi stood behind him. The person in black set the food tray down on Kevin's desk. Kevin looked up from his magazine and nodded. The person in black crossed back to the door, and it opened just enough to slip through, out of the room. The door shut and there was the harsh, metallic slide of a heavy bolt. Kevin kept bouncing his foot. He sang a line.

We are your friends.

Naomi came around beside Jake and leaned toward the screen. Her hair fell forward and she tucked it back behind her ear. Her ear stuck out a bit, the helix collapsing outward toward him. It was bright red from the cold. Jake felt an overwhelming desire to stand up and kiss her there where the cartilage looked soft, like a newborn baby bat. He felt something crunch heavy in his chest.

"I've seen some empty trays," Jake explained quickly. "Sometimes he's eating, but I've never seen how he gets food."

Jake's lips were dry, and his molars stuck to his tongue while he spoke. Naomi checked the clock count: 1,524 hours, 43 minutes, 13 seconds. She sniffed and set her mittens on the desk, and Jake felt like a creep. He saw his apartment, as Naomi did, the low ceiling, the computer monitors and the dirty couch. Jake didn't have people over often.

"He's down there all the time?"

"Yeah," Jake said. "It's this experiment."

Kevin got up out of bed and ate some food with his headphones still on, bopping his head to the music. Then he went back to the bed and flipped through his magazine.

Jake and Naomi watched the screen and Jake tried hard not to turn his head toward her, not to say anything.

He remembered seeing Naomi the night before at the Hoof. He'd run across the bar with a tea light in each hand. Tables were turned over behind him: shattered glass and hot wax covered the floor, and Marce was chasing him. He'd looked back over his shoulder and Naomi was standing with her hands at her sides. He'd lobbed a tea light across the room, over Marce's head, and it had landed at Naomi's feet, the candle extinguishing and smoke trailing up around her knees. She'd tilted her chin up and studied Jake with curiosity, like a kid standing over a worm on the sidewalk, watching it squirm in the hot sun. He'd felt like he'd been poked hard with a stick. Jake had stopped running and laughing and Marce had caught up with him. "You stupid fuck," she'd said and shoved him toward the door.

Jake flinched in real time at the memory, and Kevin pushed the tray away and took off his headphones. He moved across the White Room toward the bathroom. The screen cut to an overhead: a European-style bathroom where the toilet was in the shower and the whole room was tiled.

"Uh, that's the bathroom," Jake said.

Jake looked at Naomi and she was leaning in close with one hand resting on the desk.

"There's a chair in the kitchen," Jake said.

Kevin popped the toilet seat open and undid his pants. Naomi got a chair from the kitchen and sat down next to Jake. Kevin took a steady dump, breathing heavy through his mouth. Naomi laughed.

"This is unbelievable," she said.

She looked over her shoulder at the apartment.

"How long have you lived here?"

"A few years," Jake said.

"Just you?"

"It was a friend's place. He moved to Thailand. He left me his car too."

"Good friend," Naomi said.

Kevin flushed the toilet and the camera cut to the main room. He opened the bathroom door and went to the bed. He put his headphones back on and picked up his magazine. He lay down.

"Almost too real," Naomi said.

"Right?" Jake said.

Naomi took her phone out of her pocket and checked the time.

"I should head out," she said.

"Work?" Jake said.

"To visit my mom."

"Where's your mom?"

"Milton."

"I grew up near there."

"Oh yeah?" Naomi said.

She stood up and checked her phone again.

"The burbs," Jake said.

"No kidding."

She turned, eyes on her screen. Jake stood up.

"So, I'll see you later."

"Yeah, see you."

She let herself out and the door clicked gently behind her. The extra chair sat at the desk, an interruption in Jake's stark room. Everything else was the same, dim and untouched. But Jake felt the heat of her hand on the desk. He could smell the cold on her skin. He decided to leave the chair where it was. It was nice to pretend she was coming back to sit with him.

Jake watched Kevin turn one page and then another. He waited for Kevin to get up and talk into the camera, but he just got out of bed and started doing push-ups on the floor. Kevin counted them out loud. Twenty-four, twenty-five. He started to sweat between his shoulder blades and down his chest. Jake left the browser open and went back to bed.

❖

The tea light incident wasn't soon forgotten, and it was months before Jake was allowed back in the Hoof. He hunkered down for the winter and found ways to entertain himself at home. He stocked up on beer and Jameson and played a lot of Replay Poker on one monitor while streaming Kevin on the other. Jake drank and won at cards and Kevin doodled cartoons of skateboarding dogs, their tongues lolling in the wind.

Jake kept playing some kid from Miami. His username was TUBBYBALLS. One day, Jake got lazy and made a stupid bet, and after that Tubby won a couple of rounds in a row. Replay Poker had a chat function, which was really shit with a guy like Tubby.

TUBBYBALLS

u r a faggit

JAKE

one more game

Jake got a beer from the fridge and poured himself another whiskey. The flop came up: five of spades, king of spades, and ace of clubs. Jake had a pair of fours. Tubby bet and Jake called. Then the turn. Queen of diamonds.

TuBbYBalls

im ging to skullfuck ur mom

Tubby bet $50. Jake went in $100. Tubby called. The river came up king of diamonds. Tubby had a jack and a two.

JAKE

fucked in the butthole

TuBbYBalls

CUNT

Tubby cashed out and logged off. Jake confirmed his winnings. He finished his whiskey and got a beer from the fridge. His phone buzzed in his fleece pocket. A text from Naomi.

Hey, I can't find that guy — that see if he combusts guy.

Jake could have sent her the stream. He could have kept heckling Tubby over chat for the rest of the afternoon, finishing his case of beer. But he still had her chair set out, empty beside him, and Kevin wasn't talking much lately so he thought why not? Naomi had already seen the place. She'd seen how he lived. He texted her back.

you can't get it traditionally

The reply came back right away.

Can I come over?

Jake was a bit drunk by the time she got there. He got a beer from the fridge and offered one to Naomi. She shook her head.

"I'm going to see my mom later," she said. "It's my day off."

Jake shrugged and pulled out Naomi's chair. He cracked his beer and she sat down.

The White Room was streaming and Kevin was sleeping in the bed. He was curled up on his side, back turned to the camera. The view cut to an overhead of the room. Kevin hugged a pillow against his chest. His cheeks were flushed.

"Everyone looks like a kid when they sleep," Naomi said.

Naomi started going over to Jake's to watch Kevin on her days off. She always showed up around noon, got in a couple hours of the White Room and then went to go see her mom. Jake started getting ready for her. He would shower, brush his teeth, get dressed. He tried to get in a few drinks before Naomi got there, switching to orange juice when she came. He would pour two tall glasses and drop an ice cube into each. The ice clinked against the bottom of the glass and rose, bobbing to the surface. Jake finished his juice in two gulps. Naomi made hers last the afternoon.

Naomi watched Kevin closely. She paid a lot of attention to what he said, leaning in, hungry for more. Jake wasn't used to watching Kevin directly. Naomi started pointing out things he hadn't noticed before. The cameras always cut to the right place like they seemed to know where Kevin was going. The lights were always on. They never dimmed, even when Kevin was asleep.

Kevin stopped speaking for a while. He didn't do a single confessional. He just lay in bed, napping or scribbling his dogs in various stages of decomposition. Bugs crawled on their skulls, nibbled at their eyeballs.

"Why won't he talk?" Naomi asked Jake one afternoon.

She took a sip of her juice and wiped her mouth with the back of her hand. She rested her hand on the desk. The moist patch on her hand glistened, reflecting the white light of the monitor.

"He doesn't talk like he used to," Jake said.

"I think he's laying on an American accent," Naomi said. "Sometimes his vowels are harder. It makes it easier, story-wise, if he's American, anyway. More mass appeal. I bet he's some kind of actor. His face is very symmetrical."

"Story-wise?"

"If it's like a constructed reality thing," Naomi said. "Like LonelyGirl15 when we were in high school."

When Naomi left, Jake could still hear her voice in the apartment. He could feel her hand, glowing and wet. It lasted for hours. He tried to stick to beer after Naomi left. He didn't want to get obliterated and forget what she said to him, how she laughed at Kevin's boxers with the four-leaf clover on the crotch. How she filled the apartment like warm clutter, like things that had been collected, lovingly, over time. Postcards and bird figurines. Dog-eared paperbacks piled high up the walls. If Jake kept going hard on whiskey into the night, her voice would fade into the corners of the apart-ment and get leached up by the dark. When he woke up, he wouldn't feel her there anymore. Everything bare again.

At night, Jake stayed up late watching Kevin alone, drawing a diagram of the White Room, searching out blind spots left by the cameras. He looked for signs of construct or intervention. To see if it could be fake, if maybe Kevin didn't have to explode. But he couldn't find anything. Jake accepted the realness of the White Room as if it were his own. They were watching a dying man. But it wasn't as important for Naomi. She was just passing through. She kept her jacket slung over the back of the chair, ready for when she had to leave.

Jake and Naomi watched Kevin all winter. Jake would taper off and quit drinking. Then he'd slip up and have one, really meaning for it to be just one, but it never lasted that way. He'd dump everything out and start over.

He got really sick with a chest infection and lost weight. Naomi started bringing him fruit – clementines and kiwis – and she made tea. They sipped at it from mugs, the steam gathering moist under their noses. They didn't talk much. Neither of them was a talker.

The snow began to melt and Kevin spoke into the camera again, launching into long monologues. That's what Naomi called them, an aside to the ever-present audience. Once Kevin went on for an hour about a girl who used to babysit him when he was a kid. He never said her name, but he talked about how she lived down the street from him. He loved her. Kevin said he used to press his head up against her chest when he was little and it wasn't sexual, he knew. The hot swell of her against his temple made him feel safe.

Jake and Naomi listened to the confessional. Jake took long breaths, labouring under the mucous in his chest. He coughed, trying to bring it up, but it stuck deep. After Kevin finished talking, Jake turned to Naomi.

"You still don't think it's real?" he asked.

"I don't believe that he'll stay down there forever."

Her phone buzzed. She tugged it out of her jacket and checked the screen.

"I should get going," she said.

She stood up. What she said made Jake feel hopeful, just for a second, and he wanted to ask her to stay. But as the words formed at the back of his throat, he felt like he was swimming in mud, like there was a cold fish in his stomach, and if he just asked her to please stay a bit longer he would choke and spit up lake water all over the floor.

"I have a car," Jake said. "I can drive you."

"I'm used to the train," Naomi said.

The next day, after it was dark, Jake started for the liquor store. He left his coat unzipped. He let the cool spring wind rake down his trachea and into his lungs. He longed for Naomi; for that full, cluttered feeling she left in the apartment.

He got to the liquor store and stopped in front of the sliding doors. Inside, the aisles were sharply lit, shelves of gleaming glass bottles stretched back into the bright, cavernous recesses. In the glint of light on the bottles Jake could see Kevin's bugs. Crawling over skin, the system taking over the whole. The way circumstances worked away on their own, to bring down the dog as if he'd never ran or lived in the wild. And Jake didn't want to stay down; he wanted to live.

He knew Naomi's schedule by then, knew she would be at the Hoof. He turned around and walked east back toward the Hoof. He stood out in the cold and watched her. She looked up from the bar and saw him. He waved. She looked at him like, *What are you doing here?* but waved back with one slow swing of her arm, like a branch swaying thoughtfully in the wind. Jake didn't know how to go inside. He was used to standing still and waiting.

He remembered what it was like to be a little kid and to always be afraid of getting punched in the throat at recess. He remembered going home for lunch and his mom not being there, but crawling into his parents' bed to smell her. Dryer sheets and perfume and sweat like copper. He remembered iron blood, hot in his mouth from a tooth falling out, and crying because the neighbours were setting off fireworks and they were loud, so loud that his skull cracked and cold spread out from his chest into his fingers and toes.

He tried to speak up, to reach out for Naomi. He wanted to do something about his life. Jake turned away and walked home to the apartment. He got into bed and lay awake all night, shivering and sweating under the sheets. The sun rose, lighting up the sky pale blue. The buzzer went off and Naomi came inside.

The computer was on, as always, and Kevin was still asleep in his bed. He was curled up on his side, hugging his pillow and breathing gently through his mouth. His lips were relaxed. He sighed. Naomi stood inside the apartment with Jake facing her. He was wearing his fleece and boxers and his hair was messy and sticking up. He hadn't slept.

Jake stepped toward Naomi and her hands lifted slightly.

"Okay," Jake said. "I want to drive you to your mom's."

"You left the apartment," she said.

"Please let me drive you," Jake said again. "I'm not drinking anymore."

Naomi nodded. She crossed her arms, then let them fall to her sides. She took a step closer to Jake and he could smell lavender and fresh paper.

"You can drive me," she said.

There was a crunching sound of bed sheets from the computer speaker. Kevin rolled over in bed and sat up. He swung both feet onto the floor and looked up at the confessional cam across the room. Straight at Jake.

"Turn it off," Naomi said.

"Okay," said Jake.

Jake knew it was time to get dressed. It would be easy to stay inside with Kevin and count the days. Jake didn't know what would happen to Kevin. Maybe he would stay in the White Room forever. But he couldn't stick around to wait and see.

"Okay," he said again. He turned off the monitor.

N^AOMI

AN OPEN EYE

Jake was driving Naomi home from the hospital. They were on the road later than usual and the sun had started to set behind them. "Can we go to the creek?" Naomi said.

"Okay," Jake said.

Long fingers of light reached into the car, rubbing Naomi's shoulders pink and orange, the colour of popsicles and cream soda. Jake pulled off the highway and drove south toward the park. It had a few trail loops and a small gravel parking lot. There was a creek with picnic benches scattered along the grassy bank. Jake and Naomi got out of the car and sat down past the benches at the top of a gentle slope. They watched the water. The sun dipped lower and the sky grew dark.

"How was your mom today?" Jake said.

"She's okay," Naomi said.

Jake tried to stay full off those little exchanges. He was hungry for talk. But Naomi spoke when she was ready, and sometimes after the hospital she wasn't ready. Jake never went into the psych ward with her. He waited in the parking lot for her to finish. When she got back into the car, he tried to be really quiet for her. But that night, in the creek park, he found it hard to sit still. There were so many competing sounds, the flush of wind in the trees and the trickle of water over rocks. He could make out the distant rumble of the highway, the concerned yelp of a dog on the park trails. He started to worry about going back home, about what would happen after he dropped Naomi off. He didn't want to be alone.

Naomi leaned back and slipped her hands into the grass. She tilted her head back and gazed up over the tree line on the opposite bank. Toronto rose beyond the trees, a steel promise of forever. A yellow fog hung low around the buildings, beating up into the black, overcast sky.

Jake could feel the city leaning in over them, he could hear the streets and the car squeals. The rushed spill of feet over the sidewalk when the bars emptied out for the night. The screech of the subway tracks and the transit workers screaming at people to move back, move back to make room. And then Jake got thirsty. He got thirsty and wished he still had a bottle in the car. He leaned forward and wound his hands through his hair. He pulled hard at his scalp so he wouldn't think of everything he'd dumped down the drain in his apartment or how many days he had sober on that stupid counter on his phone. He tried not to think about going home and being alone in the rooms where he'd done all his bad things. He could see the burn-scarred kitchen counter, the girl on his computer with the bogus smile and the thick bangs. How the walls behind her were peeling yellow, and she talked dirty like it was rehearsed, like it was practiced, because it was, and she happened to laugh, the only real-sounding thing in the video, right when Jake came.

Naomi stood up. She stretched up to the sky, reaching with every finger. Her chest puffed up full and she let go of a long breath. It escaped from her mouth, a low moan draining out toward the yellow city light. It filled the dark space between the creek and the skyscrapers. When her chest emptied flat and her voice trailed off hoarse, she sat down again. Naomi pulled her knees up to her chest and crossed her arms.

It felt like she had grazed the inside of his wrist with her index finger. He shivered, the invisible touch passing warm between them. They had started to share quiet intimacies like that. They'd started to unwind in front of each other, almost forgetting the other person was there. Sometimes he'd catch himself humming, something he did when he was a kid. Something he'd forgotten he did.

Jake cleared his throat and looked down. A caterpillar, its back feathery brown like eyelashes, crept across the rubber toe of his sneaker.

"Naomi," Jake whispered.

She turned to look and rested her chin on her crossed forearms, her whole body balled up tight like a little kid. They sat while the caterpillar passed over Jake's shoe and stepped lightly into the grass. It slipped into the cross-hatched canopy of green and disappeared.

"I haven't seen a caterpillar in so long," Jake said.

Jake had been seeing a lot of small things lately. A kid's Velcro sneaker in the gutter. The thread where a button had come loose from his shirt. The scum line in his bathtub. The world felt loud and it made him want to cry.

"When was the last time?" Naomi said, leaning toward him.

"Probably when I was a kid. You know, playing in the dirt?"

She nodded and closed her eyes.

"Can you tell me?"

"Okay," Jake said.

He crossed his legs, careful to avoid the place where the caterpillar had crawled under the grass.

"I was with someone in our backyard," Jake said. "Maybe it was one of the neighbour kids."

Naomi nodded.

"It was weird, actually. I was by myself just for a couple minutes on the deck. And I saw this bug; it was totally see-through and its back was like clear jelly. It didn't have any hair. Not like this one."

Jake spoke and Naomi stayed facing him with her head resting on her knees. She kept her eyes closed, nodding seriously, prompting him for more. Like a steady magician pulling bright, silk scarves out of his throat: yellow, red, green.

"No one believed me," Jake said. "But I could see all of its organs, these bloody and brown pockets inside of it. Its eyes were totally black."

Naomi opened her eyes and Jake kept talking. He talked about all the bugs he had seen as a kid. Snails stuck to leaves in a bush on the way to school. He collected them and kept them in a yogurt container. He didn't remember what happened to them. A hundred spiders in a willow tree at school. A kid climbed up and screamed when he found them. A praying mantis snapping a bee out of the air. It ate the bee's body until all that was left was the head, its long pink tongue stuck out all the way, like it was about to lick a frozen street lamp.

"I'm afraid to go home," Jake said. "To be alone with myself."

Naomi nodded.

"All I want is to go home," she said.

They talked the whole way back to Toronto. They talked to remind one another, without touching, that they were still there. They talked about lost gloves, and how they wanted to visit the mountains, and the kitten Naomi had for a while when she was younger. They had to give the kitten away, she explained, because her dad was allergic.

They talked and they exited off the highway, taking Spadina north through the city.

"Do you want to stay with me?" Naomi said. "I have a couch. It's like a futon."

They edged past condo buildings in traffic. Every light in every building was lit.

"Okay," Jake said.

"Are you hungry?"

"Not really," Jake said.

"Me either."

They stopped at a red light, nightwalkers slipping in front of the car, their backs erect, eyes turning sharply over the road.

"My dad used to ask me all the time if I wanted food," Naomi went on. "Whenever my mom was sick, that's all he ever asked me. Are you hungry? Are you sure? He would make so much food."

Jake held his breath. He didn't want her to stop. The light turned green and they moved uptown.

"I remember he took me for a hot chocolate the first time she was in the hospital."

They passed dumpling houses and noodle shops. People inside sipped tea and lifted steaming bowls to their mouths.

They turned up onto Naomi's street. She had a tiny bachelor on the second floor of a house. Jake parked and killed the engine. They sat and Jake felt empty. In a good way. It was like he had gorged himself for so long and finally been sick. He felt like he could sleep. Waves of dull, fluttering silence filled the car.

Jake reached across the car and took Naomi's hand. She ran a fingertip along the inside of his wrist. He wasn't afraid. Naomi breathed steady beside him. And they sat in stillness, comfortable at last in that miraculously clear first touch.

WE FIND DYNAMITE, NOT GOLD

"Look, Naomi," my mother whispered one afternoon as she came into the kitchen. "Do you remember these?"

She was cradling two ceramic jugs in her arms. One had a chip in the handle and the other was purple-stained from wine. Lines notched the inside like rings on a tree. I couldn't place them.

"They're nice, Mom," I said from the kitchen table. It was covered in old photo albums she'd put out for me to look at.

"We used to have parties with these," she said.

She drifted around the table and set the pitchers on the floor by the back door, pausing to dress each with a sprig of goldenrod. She had all kinds of weeds drying out on the counter, collected from the backyard. My mother moved slowly, with ceremony. Everything meant something to her; everything was precious.

She came up behind me and patted my back.

"Pretty?" she said.

"Yes," I said. She kissed my cheek.

"I'm going to paint."

She disappeared upstairs to the studio and I listened for the click of the sliding door before I went up after her to my room. Mugs of tea and empty plates sat forgotten on every other stair. I was visiting for the night, had just arrived off the train and caught a cab to the house. It looked like she'd been spending a lot of time inside. Boxes lined the hallways, dragged up from the garage or the basement. Collage projects gathered on the walls, held up by thumbtacks and Scotch tape. I walked past them and they shivered like colourful feathers

Upstairs in the bedrooms, the beige walls were covered with framed family pictures. There I was: two, seven, 11, 14. With a gap-tooth, with braces, with lip gloss too orange, and awkward shoulders like gargoyle wings. Basketball teams and swimming in Lac Ouiment. And sometimes my dad was there beside me. Hands on his hips, gangly in athletic shorts and a ball cap.

The door to my room was open. There was a stack of children's books and a banker's box sat in the middle of the floor. Everything else was the same as the day I'd moved out. The bed was covered in the white duvet with blue daisies. The headboard was plastered with Daffy Duck stickers, turning yellow and flaking at the edges like lace. I slept in that bed, my feet nearly clearing the end, until I was 18. There was an empty corkboard up on the wall and a window overlooking the side yard, some garbage cans, and the air conditioner. The closet was padded with all my old winter jackets and basketball jerseys.

A paper bag in the middle of the bed had been cut into long strips and coloured with green and blue markers. There were two googly eyes attached at the top and my name was scratched at the edge in red crayon. It was supposed to be a squid puppet, I think. I must have made it when I was small. To my mother, the bag, like everything else, was important. Maybe it was the first time I glued on whole circles or conquered the A in my name. It didn't matter. If I left her, she would have happily buried herself in that house, sorting everything into piles like a crow.

I slipped the bag over my hand and moved its mouth in three long gasps. I pulled it off and crushed it into a ball. I grabbed the box on the floor. Inside there was a bundle of birthday cards, a deflated balloon, a ball of grey yarn and a half-finished cable-knit sock. I put the children's books and the crumpled puppet in the box and snuck back downstairs and out the front door.

I went to the end of our street and turned onto the boulevard, heading for the bridge and the public ravine trail where there was a metal garbage bin. I dropped the box in and it landed with a hollow clunk against the bottom. It made barely a dent in the clutter but it felt real. Like I'd done something she couldn't.

I visited as much as I could. I took afternoons or weekends off, as much time as I could get away from work. I brought her groceries and cooked puréed soups to freeze and defrost. Maybe it felt like a lot because my dad was gone. Maybe he'd been shielding me from the responsibility all those years and only then was I seeing the full force of it: the curtains drawn on the main floor, the clutter rising around her ankles with all the ferocity of white water rapids.

She saw a family doctor who wore high leather boots and seemed to prefer delivering babies over follow-up visits. The doctor had pictures of newborns tacked up on the walls of her waiting room, wrinkled little hands and faces. The doctor never let me sit in on an appointment. "I read about lithium…?" I said once over my mom's shoulder, trying to push in after her into the exam room. "Your mother is a grown woman," the doctor said, smiling and holding up her hand. "She'll see you in the waiting room when we're all done."

Sometimes they would tinker with a dose or try a new pill and my mom would get a burst of clarity where two meds would react well together or the absence of one would allow her to feel the full effects of another. Other times, I'd get home and find her in the studio chattering to a wall or staring out the rear kitchen window into the ravine, holding a pillow to her chest. I didn't know much about the chemistry of her illness. She'd try to explain how she felt and then falter and give up. *It's like how you see things in dreams without the cloudiness. It's like a voice in your ear that's not saying anything.* The pitchers and the puppet bothered me. It felt like she was trying to show me something.

I cut back across the street toward the house. I kicked off my shoes and went right upstairs to the studio. I rolled the door open, so it slid back into the wall. My mother was smearing red paint on a giant canvas with a gas station squeegee. I decided not to ask how she got it. She was working over a drop sheet, at least. There were two more canvases leaning against the far wall, the top corners were beaten up from being dragged out of the garage and slammed up the stairs. The studio ceiling was high, but her really big canvases were supposed to stay downstairs in the dining room, so they didn't get damaged. The dining room was meant to be studio spillover, but she hated the light.

"Mom," I said.

"I hate that light," she said, with her back to me.

"That's because you close the curtains."

"The neighbours can see right in," she said.

She shook her head and kept squeegeeing. The paint squeaked on the canvas. The excess slid down her arm and dripped off her elbow like candle wax.

I rolled the studio door shut. My dad had done the renovation on the attic when I was little. I remember him wearing canvas pants with a bandana tied around his forehead like a pirate. He always did work around the house on the weekends. The house was his hobby. He put in stairs and installed a ventilation system.

I flicked on the hood vent and waited for the fans to rev up. She said the noise distracted her, but I couldn't have her high on paint fumes. I went back downstairs, collecting mugs and plates on the way. The main floor was dedicated to my parents' private collection, pieces purchased at auctions or traded with friends over the years. Smaller sculptures filled every surface. My mother's paintings mingled nicely throughout. She really knew how to stage a room, once. When I was a kid, her agent got the house featured in some design magazine. In the spread, my mother sat in a high-backed chair, unsmiling, her chin level at the camera, her hair cropped short just under her ear. Now there were tables pushed up under every wall, piled high with mail and newspapers and magazines and jars of paper clips. Underneath, she'd stuff boxes rummaged from the basement and the garage, the tape picked open, the wedding china held up and examined so she could remember what kind of pink the flowers were on the pattern.

Sometimes I'd find a box of my dad's stuff, labelled in my mother's writing like he would be sending for them any day now. "Good riddance," I'd whisper, shoving a box with the ball of my foot. Then I'd feel bad. So, he'd left. Who could blame him?

My mother took up side projects: collages when she was stable, and the occult when she wasn't. She collected tarot decks and crystals, blue quartz to balance her mood. She painted when she was working through a big idea, lost thoughts and hard questions. Painting usually signalled there was about to be some great upheaval.

I learned the rhythms of her days. Her eyes turned pale blue in the evening, like all the energy had been bled out of her. She paced. She slept all the time or not at all. She used to put more effort into leaving the house, but it always seemed to end poorly, with her on hands and knees in the front hall, gasping for air, having been set off by a helicopter in the sky. Her car stayed parked in the garage and gathered dust. I thought about selling it, but hoped, quietly, that she'd get better one day and be able to use it again. Her agent had canvases and supplies delivered; the guy who dropped them off knew the code to get into the garage. Sometimes he'd take a piece with him, only if she left it there. He probably never even saw her. He probably thought she was crazy, a bona fide recluse.

I carried my armful of dishes to the kitchen and set them beside the sink. I ran the water hot and started to work my way through the pile of pots and pans. I moved slowly through the stack, uncovering apple cores and orange peels as I went. I collected organics in a paper towel and bundled them up, ready for compost. The bin was under the sink. The smell of rot hit me as soon as I opened the cupboard.

The compost was overflowing; the bag had split from the wet weight of it all. I wondered, not for the first time, why she insisted on composting if she couldn't keep up with it. It would be easier if she just had garbage, no recycling, no anything. She struggled to get the bins out to the curb. One day was enough to remember, never mind two or three different pickups.

I pulled everything out and scrubbed the cabinet with bleach until my nose burned.

"I'll do that," she said behind me.

I looked up over my shoulder. Her hands were red at her sides. Wet and shiny. For a second, I thought it was blood, that she'd mangled herself somehow with a palette knife. Fear rushed down my arms, an electric blue current shot into my fingertips. Then I remembered the paint and the squeegee. It was too red, anyway, hyper-real like in *Carrie*. Blood was different. A sort-of brown, like it came from the earth.

"I don't want you to," she said.

She sat down cross-legged on the floor behind me. She was wearing a big white shirt and leggings. She put her wet hands in her lap.

"I got it, Mommy."

"Did you see your puppet? What a treasure."

I loved her, of course. A throbbing, ache of a love, constant and unknowable like peristalsis. Sometimes it would come over me in waves, like there on the kitchen floor, the adrenaline still sharp in my hands. I could see her trying to piece together where she went wrong. Her eyes searching mine, slipping back and forth quickly over my face like a child who'd made a mess. She felt bad.

I knew what the puppet meant then. Like, see? Look what I found. You were little once and we were happy. Right? Please tell me we were.

I wanted to crawl into her lap and say, "Hey, Mommy, that's okay, everything's fine." But neither of us really would have believed that. Because she couldn't be my mother anymore. Not really.

I helped her wipe her hands on a rag, then lead her to the big sink in the laundry room. I washed her, squeezing soap over her hands and arms, lathering up to her elbows. She was small but strong. I turned the water warm and she closed her eyes. The water ran pink down the drain.

I sat her down at the kitchen table and cleared a space. I took out her collage scraps. Magazines and children's scissors, glue sticks and a piece of bristol board. I sat down across from her and we got to work sticking bits of paper together. She hummed softly across from me.

There was something intangible there. Something big. The apology, a transaction we couldn't manage to have. *I'm sorry, Naomi. It's okay, Mom.* And I wanted it to be.

And there were the real things, the things we could have: the house, her new painting, different kinds of red to chat about, and the pearls in a magazine that would go perfectly on our collage. There was pasta with asparagus and mushrooms for dinner, sautéed in a pan and topped with parsley. There was my old bed to collapse into, exhausted, arms heavy, when the night came. There were weird, worried dreams. There was a way to thrash and moan and almost fall out onto the floor like I was four again. Then, there were her hands on my back, steady like a lake on a calm summer night. There was her weight on the bed beside me, the give and creak of the mattress, and her voice hushing me back to sleep.

WHAT SHE HAD YOU FOR

I went over to the house to help my mother move some paintings up from the basement. That was where her archive lived: the only part of the house that stayed neat, where my dad's systems still lived in full. There were wood floors, pot lights, and rows and rows of canvases wrapped in paper and separated by narrow posts. There were a few cabinets with thin drawers labelled by year, stuffed full of drawings and studies, plastic containers stacked high with overflow. The basement smelled like packing tape and old paper. The archive, I always thought, was the greatest proof of my dad's love for my mother. To him, she always made sense, as an artist. To him, she was a talent worthy of preservation.

My mother didn't like spending time in the basement, being afraid of underground places in general, so I went and pulled the pieces she'd asked for from a photorealistic series she'd done in the early Nineties, called *Afterbirth*. The larger pieces had all sold but the two of the smaller ones, maybe four feet by five, were down in the basement, tagged meticulously with titles and years scratched in David's hand. *Naomi IV 1993, Naomi II 1992.* I carried them, one at a time up the stairs where she waited for me on the first landing.

"Thanks, thanks," she said, helping me with them.

We set the pieces down in the front hallway. It was dark; she never turned the lights on and she kept the shutters closed and the curtains drawn, so only the most meagre crack of daylight came through into the house. She'd always struggled with migraines and sensitivity to light, and her headaches were a big part of my life growing up. Since I moved out, I found the dark of the house startling. There was dampness, too, lingering in the rooms as if someone had left the shower running on hot and forgotten about it.

"I can't remember which is which," Joanne said. She picked at the wrapping on one of the canvases.

"What do you need them for?"

"A show. MC called about it. She wants the whole series."

"Mom, that's great."

MC was a curator. My mother's only ever show in Toronto was with MC. *Afterbirth* was popular when I was little. I remember MC would come over a lot to stay up late and chat with my parents. She drove a boxy Mercedes from the Seventies and wore black silk suits. Her hair was spiky short and grey and she wore blue glasses. She never aged. She wasn't married and didn't have any children. She ran in the right circles in Toronto, which gave her a certain edge in selling my mother's work. She knew all the gallery owners and restaurateurs and bankers and their wives. The wives always wanted Joanne's paintings. When I was a bit older, my mother started to struggle with her mind and she had a hard time concentrating on work. We saw MC less and less, but when she did come over, she'd hold my face in her palms for a moment, her hands soft and cool, and she would study how I'd aged, turning my face ever so slightly from left to right. "Just as I thought," she'd say. "Your mother's twin."

Joanne tore back the wrapping on the first canvas. Underneath the painting was all blue, a low angle looking up at a baby, teetering precariously at the top of a flight of stairs. Visually it was quite striking, the blues vivid and hyper-real, everything sharp, the angles slanted and stretching toward the baby at the top of the stairs. It gave you the same feeling as an optical illusion might, so you experienced the visual trick of the thing. The baby was just a baby, after all. It wasn't so otherworldly, so terrifying.

It was easy to feel separate from the painting, even though it was of me. The whole *Afterbirth* series felt like it was from another person's life. While some of my earliest memories were of my mother painting my face up in the studio, six feet high and bright pink, contorted like the insides of a conch shell, I think I became too used to the shock of it. I remember some friends being like, *Wow, that's how your mother sees you?* But I shrugged it off. It's a postpartum series, I told them. About the struggle of motherhood.

"This one's good," I said.

"Maybe," she said.

Joanne crossed her arms and tilted her head to the side. She was slow and, on her meds, then. Living very much in reality, wearing cotton sweatpants and a white T-shirt.

"It's good, Mom," I said again.

I was tired that day. I'd worked a long shift the night before. I'd closed up and walked halfway home before I realized I'd forgotten my wallet on the bar by the cash, so I had to double back in the snow to get it. By the time I made it to my bed I collapsed, my muscles aching, but I couldn't fall asleep.

I got like that sometimes, if I stayed awake for too long, my brain weighing every little thing I'd said to the customers, shuddering at how I nearly sent a pint glass flying with my elbow. Sleep was a training I never received in full. I'd always been a bad sleeper. I'd gotten used to staying up really late for work and taking a Benadryl when I got home, chasing it with whiskey and tea. But when I read an article about kids mixing over the counter shit with drinking and how that was sending my generation's livers into shock by the time we were 30, I decided not to do that anymore.

I gave my mother a hug, pressing my hands flat against her back, checking, out of habit, to see if she'd been eating. She was pointy, still slightly underweight, but her hair was clean. It smelled like rosemary and mint. She pulled back and forced a smiled up at me.

"How are you feeling?" I said.

"Oh, you know," she said.

"Day by day."

She nodded.

"Do you want a tea?" she asked.

"Sure."

I followed her into the kitchen. The house was neater than usual, a good sign, but the drawn curtains made everything feel solemn, like the house was veiled in mourning. It reminded me of the dark parts of forests, where the ground was always wet, and the things that grew didn't need light, like moss, and mushrooms, and salamanders.

Joanne put the kettle on. The table was busy with magazines and scrap paper. She had a *Vogue* open and a small pile of mouths cut out from the magazine. Huge white teeth, a wet pink tongue, a waxy moustache. When she was slow like that – readjusting to her medications, finding balance again – small busy tasks like collages helped keep her hands occupied. I think she learned that once from the hospital. I never remember her doing crafts before then. When I was in grade school, I thought she was too good for those stupid arts and crafts projects they made the patients do. She was a real artist, what did she need a colouring book for? Truth was, she loved them. Finding and making patterns soothed her, like the repetition of a nursery rhyme. Cats in the cradle, baby bunnies with velvet noses, and a moon made of cheese.

"Will you go to the show?" I asked as I sat down at the table.

"I'm not sure," she said. She took out two mugs from the cupboard.

"It's in Toronto, right? Maybe I could meet you?"

"Maybe, Naomi, maybe."

Beside the mouths in the middle of the table there was a coiled silver chain strung with pink polished gemstones.

"That's pretty," I said.

Joanne came to my side and stroked my hair.

"Oh, my pendulum."

She picked the chain up off the table and poured it into her hand. It sat curled up on itself like a snake, the pink stones glowing on the top like eyes.

"It's jewellery?" I said.

"Not really."

She held out her hand and let the chain fall. She pinched the end between her fingers, so the stones dangled in the air, suspended inside a thin metal loop. The pendulum rotated willfully, in big circles at first before narrowing tighter, as if fixing its mind on a particular word. I shivered. The house was cold.

"Ask it a question," my mother said.

"Mom," I said.

I wasn't sure about this kind of game. She'd always been drawn to the occult: tarot and Ouija and once, when I was in grade five, I got home and there was a Reiki healer burning sage and chanting in the living room. For her, it seemed to fill the gap left by religion. These games provided answers. The pendulum swung back and forth, and the metal loop rotated around the stones as if in orbit, turning about the solar system. There was always a mental calculation that took place with these small games. Was it worth it? Was it dangerous? She was doing so well. The house was clean. She was getting paintings together for a show.

"Come on," she urged. "It will swing side-to-side for 'yes' and front-to-back for 'no.'"

The level keel of sanity wasn't enough for my mother. I knew her; she needed more. She needed something special. Something like magic, something that bound all things together. She needed the immortal soul and energy fields and chakras. That was what made her different from the rest of us. She'd gone crazy and seen magic. So now, she believed in it.

My mother tilted her head and watched the pendulum, her eyes milky, slipping out of focus.

I reached out and snapped the chain from her hand. The pink stones bounced in the air.

"Don't do that," I said.

Her eyes met mine, back in focus, startled for a second. Then she looked down, ashamed. I'd caught her misbehaving. She wasn't supposed to play. She was supposed to live in the world with me.

"Okay, "she whispered.

She sat at the table. I could feel her anguish like it was my own. But she couldn't feel me. She couldn't feel the train ride on me, feel the bodies too close together in forced air, she couldn't smell my breath, fruity and sweet from too many drinks on my shift even though I wasn't supposed to be drinking. She couldn't understand how lonely I was, how much I wanted someone in my bed at night, to kiss my eyes when they were closed. How much her and my dad's love had set me up for disappointment. Their love made me an orphan. I'd never find a home like ours again. If she understood, if she sensed me at all, she wouldn't have a pendulum. She'd be here, in the dull grey house with me.

The kettle shrieked and I put the pendulum down on the table. I filled the two mugs she'd set aside for us. The portable phone was out on the counter beside her phone book. She still kept a phone book, stuffed full of cards and notes scribbled and tucked between the pages. There were little notes scrawled with positive little affirmations and reminders, stuck to the cabinets, to the fridge. *Call Naomi. I need the medication so I can be well. Independence. A good day is one with your feet on the floor.* I carried the two mugs of tea over to the table and sat down across from my mother. She was doodling with a black ballpoint pen on a sheet of red construction paper. Crooked lines swerving into ovals. Her hands didn't work like they used to. The antipsychotics made her muscles seize up when she least expected it. She couldn't focus. She used to spend hours drawing perfect circles. She'd hold a brush or a pen steady, like a wand or a knife.

"Tell me about the show," I said.

"Okay," she said.

She reached for her mug, dunking the teabag in and out. Dark brown storm clouds gathered in the water.

"It's an exhibition of female artists," she said. "Emerging and established. So, there will be some young people there. You know MC, she's good meeting young people."

"Cool," I nodded.

She never went to many shows. When she did, she was always with my dad. He knew how to help her tour a room, knew when to get her back into the car; when she was tired of shaking hands. He spoke for her; he was her guide to the real world. She was frail in busy rooms, close to some kind of psychic tipping point. Like someone had set her toes on a cliff edge and forced her to hold a cocktail napkin and nibble on canapés. She wasn't made for conversations about the weather.

I wanted things to be right between us. I wanted to be that person for her. A guide. I could do it, I thought. She blew on her tea. Tendrils of steam rose and twisted in her hair, as if tugging her down, deeper into the dark, away from me.

"I'm sorry," I cried, half jumping across the table, scrambling for her hand.

My mother leaned forward to meet me. She reached for my hand and squeezed it.

"What for?"

"Let's ask the pendulum," I said.

"What?"

"If we'll go to the show?"

"Oh. Really?"

"Just for fun, okay?"

"Okay," she said, squeezing my hand again.

We stood like witches in the kitchen. My mother let the pendulum swing out in front of her.

"We have to think of the question in our head," she said. "Don't say it out loud."

I nodded. The pendulum rotated in wide circles before narrowing in the air. My mother's face was calm, serene, like a figurehead cut in the likeness of Aphrodite or the Oracle at Delphi. I wondered if she was asking something different from me, if she was thinking about the show at all.

The pendulum settled on a straight motion, front to back, over and over. My mother's face cracked into a smile, it stretched all the way up to her eyes, breaking the fog in the grey of the kitchen.

"It's a 'yes,'" she said.

"So we'll go?"

"Yes."

❖

The night of the show we planned to meet at the gallery. MC had a car sent to the house to get Joanne, and I lived just a couple blocks away. It was an old industrial stretch behind Bloor Street that had suddenly turned chic in the 2000s. Now it was all restaurants and breweries and artisanal leather shops. There was a white poster in the front window of the gallery with WOMEN IN ART printed in big, glossy black letters. The blue painting from *Afterbirth* was in the front window. I went inside and gave the girls at the front my name. They ushered me into the packed, vaulted room. The walls were pristine and white and rose up forever under a grey ceiling made of interlocking metal beams. I left my winter things at the coat check. People holding glasses of wine chatted in tight groups. I was underdressed in jeans and a plain black sweater. I slipped past girls slung in vintage rabbit fur, their lips curled up, sardonic and wet with purple and orange gloss. I craned my neck over the crowd. The rest of *Afterbirth* was hanging in the back of the gallery. Nine pieces, each done in their own colour. Red, purple, orange and green, my face twisted in a howl, or thoughtful and conciliatory, still wet with tears.

I started toward them and felt a hand on my bicep. I turned around to face MC. She'd shrunk over the years, but her hair was still grey and pointy as icicles. She cupped my face in her hands.

"Your mother is on her way," she said. "I sent a car."

"Yes, thank you," I said.

She turned my face gently to the right and then let her hands drop away. Her fingers left cool impressions on my cheeks, wet spots on a foggy windowpane.

"Come," she said.

She pulled me toward the back of the gallery. There was a bar to the left of my mother's work. MC set me up with the guy pouring drinks.

"Give her whatever she wants," she shouted over the brutal drum of the crowd. She touched my cheek one last time and then left my side. I watched her spiky head bob and weave in between bodies. Feathered hats, knitted pocket squares and eyebrows creamy with ink. A man in an acid-green tailcoat laughed too hard and started to cough. Someone slapped him on the back and handed him a Scotch. MC popped up on the other side of the gallery, near a raised platform opposite the bar. There was a podium and a thick black microphone.

I ordered a rum and Coke and stared up at the collective *Afterbirth*, like it had always hung in that big white room, as a whole, all those giant snapshots frozen one after the other in succession. It was fortunate they got all the pieces for the show. The progression of time made an impact. The terrible exhaustion of my mother's red newborn weeks, positioned beside her melancholic toddler blues. I could study it with the clinical detachment of my ensuing decades. That was the thing about growing up and looking back on yourself as a baby: it felt like someone else's life.

There was a shift in the crowd near the door. I saw my mother come in through the entrance, shed her coat, and pass it to a girl at the coat check. She swept through the gallery like a solemn, spinning top, wearing all black, her mouth painted red in a hard line. I knew it was her, but she was different. She was wearing the silver pendulum strung around her neck. In her eyes, I could see she was living magic. She'd stopped taking her medication. The crowd parted ways for her and she drifted past them, her gaze fixed forward.

I stayed at the bar, frozen.

"Another one?" the bartender asked. I was gripping the empty glass in my hand.

I nodded and he fixed me another. I drank it fast. My mother was talking to the man in green tails across the room. She laughed, a girlish sound, like glass shattering. The man laughed too. To him she was enigmatic, eccentric. I was afraid of a scene, of her saying she could feel his dead wife there in the room with him. My heart was tight with danger. The bartender set another drink beside me and I took it. When I turned around she was there, up close. She was that violent kind of perfect, her skin bright and bare. She met my eyes with a stubborn, raised chin, leaned forward and kissed me hard on the lips. I felt that I was meeting the woman that made *Afterbirth* for the first time.

"Mom," I said.

She spun around and left me at the bar, like an unwanted visitor. She left behind a strange smell I didn't recognize on her, like blue moss and sea salt. She was dark, and elegant, and I didn't know her at all. We never really know our mothers.

I looked up at one of the purple paintings in *Afterbirth*, a close shot of my face resting on my dad's shoulder. My hair stuck up fuzzy and my eyes were round, fighting sleep. I felt my mother's lips, the assault still warm on my mouth, and I wondered if she liked me at all. If I was just the object of her imprisonment; the reason for her collapse. She wasn't cut out for mothering, probably. She'd chronicled her struggle, the grotesque cry of her newborn, how it disturbed her. And that baby was me. That night, when my mother was insane, when she wore all black and spun through the gallery, she let me see what I'd kept her from being. Bold and beautiful, someone fantastic, someone admired, who people were drawn to. I hated her like that. I didn't recognize her like that.

MC appeared at the podium, her smooth voice asking the audience to gather for a couple of remarks on the show. She spoke of the vitality of woman in the Arts. How the city was a place for women's voices. How the gallery was proud to exhibit new and established artists at varying stages of their career.

My mother returned to my side. I kept my eyes down. The drinks were starting to hit me and the room felt like it was expanding, like the ceiling was rising up to the heavens. My mother wobbled beside me. She clasped her hands and looked down, as if to steady herself. Like she was on the edge of that cliff, afraid in a busy room. I wanted to reach for her hand, but I didn't.

MC's speech turned to my mother and *Afterbirth*. How in the paintings we see ourselves: child and mother, bound up in eternal conflict over love and freedom. Torment and domesticity. Purpose and loneliness.

My mother sighed and I looked up at her. Her forehead was crumpled with concern, her neck withered and white. She looked old then, still so unlike my mother, but she'd swung rapidly to the other extreme. I reached for her hand and she let me hold it. The truth was she could make magic, though I'd never tell her that. We had an extrasensory bond. I could feel her from a distance. I loved her in a way that wasn't human, wasn't normal. It was like grabbing infinite black space and squeezing it between my palms so I could bite into it like an apple and taste stars collapsing. I wanted her to see that. I was her magic. I was enough. She'd made her love for me into something other people could understand and touch. The pain of first motherhood. The anguish of being needed, for real, for the first time in her life.

She could hate me, I thought. That was okay. We needed each other. And sometimes I hated her too.

"Now, I'd like to invite Joanne to the stage," MC said. "She'll say a few remarks on the series and then we'll get back to our cocktails."

The crowd chuckled. They were bloated and satisfied. There was applause. MC looked out over the crowd, one hand over her brow shielded her eyes from the lights overhead. Beside me, my mother let go of my hand and fingered the pendulum over her chest with a soft hand. In that second of uncertainty, I saw time switch on her, and from her dark, elevated post, she fell. She always did.

She bowed her head under the weight of a frantic mind without routine, without nursery rhymes and aphorisms and tea. I felt her change in the gallery while everyone clapped and MC said her name again over the microphone.

"Let's go," I said. She nodded.

I linked my arm through hers and led her through the crowd to the door. I grabbed our coats and we went outside into the night. I didn't know where the hired car was, so I led her down the street, in the freezing cold, both of our jackets still bunched under my arm, until we got to my apartment. I took her up the back stairs and tucked her into my bed with all of her clothes on. I got in beside her and she put her head on my shoulder. I stroked her hair and felt paint in it, tangled and matted. I recognized her again. At one point she slipped the pendulum off from around her neck and coiled it in my hand.

"Take it away from me," she whispered.

"I will," I said.

CRACKER JACKS FOR MISFITS

When I was eight, I thought my mother was turning into something like a ghost. I kind of supported the idea; she didn't embarrass me then, and I believed in spirits and magic, and New Age witches. I believed she could probably commune with another world, and how that was really special. It made her like an oracle woman from one of my books. Every day in the summer she put on a long blue kaftan that hung around her body like smoke and she moved, increasingly, like a much older woman, tender and fragile.

One morning in September, a Saturday, just after starting back at school, she came down to breakfast, her bare feet padding softly on the stairs, and sat at the table across from me. She didn't like noise in the morning, so I sat very still, sipping my orange juice without a sound.

My dad, David, whistled at the stove. He put a thick pat of butter on every pancake and piled them up in three crooked stacks. He served them and sat himself down.

"Eat up, Naomi," he said.

Joanne stared down at her plate. The butter melted and pooled in an oily moat. Up close, I could see she had specks of dried paint in her hair.

I took a quiet bite. The pancakes weren't cooked all the way through, and they stuck flat and gluey to the top of my mouth.

"How's that?" David said.

He was wearing his casual clothes, bleach-stained shorts and an old T-shirt. He was taking time off work then, and I didn't much like having him involved in our days. He made things noisy, sort of forceful. Like, for instance, we would never have eaten breakfast at the table if he wasn't around. But I didn't want to hurt his feelings so I swallowed the bite of pancake. It slid heavy into my belly.

"How's that?" David said.

I smiled and drank my whole glass of orange juice. I smacked my lips and said, *ahh*, like I'd seen kids do in breakfast commercials. Joanne flinched.

"Eat up," David said. "You're going to need energy today."

I was selling treats door-to-door for a Clovers overnight camping trip. We were going to Rouge Park. Clovers was David's idea. He said I was really shy and it would be good to work on making friends with other girls. He wanted me to sleep in a tent, eat s'mores, and spot a blue heron taking flight at dawn over a creek or a river. He wanted me to have a normal childhood, out of the house.

Joanne was an artist and an intellectual, and the kind of person other people would dress up to meet for the first time. She was beautiful, too. At that age, I loved to sit with her in the studio and watch her work, sculpting colour over canvas. The studio was in the attic, a romantic, imaginative place for any kid, like a cellar or a tree house. The room was shaped like a long triangular prism and the back window took up the whole wall. It looked over the backyard and the forest on the other side of their fence. The studio always smelled like Joanne: warm soap and packing paper.

David nudged the plate of pancakes toward Joanne before tucking into his own stack. I waited for him to notice that the pancakes weren't cooked, and say, "No one has to eat these!" and throw them all away. But instead he went *mmm* and rubbed his belly.

Joanne was still staring down at the pancakes, but she wasn't really seeing them. She was somewhere else: her head up the studio, or the backyard, or in the clouds talking to spirits. I wanted to crawl under the table, lift up her kaftan, and press my face against her belly like I used to when I was little. Joanne hadn't been feeling well for a while. She always had a hard time in September. That's why David was taking time off work. He woke up really early every morning and made these big breakfasts. Joanne never made big breakfasts. Just oatmeal or toast and tea.

David finished his pancakes.

"We should get going. What do you say, Naomi?"

"Okay."

"That's the spirit. Jo, wish us luck?"

She lifted her head.

"Good luck," she whispered.

Her eyes were dark, small and not like hers at all. Her neck was skinny and her skin was almost see-through, like a baby bird I'd found dead in the backyard once. It must have fallen out of its nest. I didn't like how small the bird was, how easily I missed it in the grass. I nearly stepped on it barefoot; its neck broken, twisted at an impossible angle, eyes cloudy black.

David loaded the big brown boxes of treats into the car. I had a clipboard with the Clovers treat sales pitch I was supposed to memorize and say at every door. I also had brochures for Clovers to hand out with treats. The girls in the brochure wore their hair in braids. The way they smiled up from the glossy paper made me nervous. Their mouths were big and their teeth were sharp at the edges like broken seashells.

We drove up the boulevard and over a few streets. David parked on the corner.

"Let's start here," he said.

We got out of the car and I put on my yellow and green Clovers beret.

David opened the trunk and checked the brown boxes.

"Okay, ready?" he grinned.

I nodded.

"Don't chew your lip. It's going to go great."

I turned toward the first house on the block. It was a normal house, just a bungalow with a green front door. The front curtains were drawn and something flickered for a second in the window, but when I looked harder there was nothing.

"Go on." David gave me a tiny push forward.

I started, tentatively up the driveway for the green door. My heart was pounding. Had I seen a ghost in the window? Away from my mother the idea of spirits didn't seem so safe. She wasn't there to protect me. At the front step I glanced back at David. He flashed me a double thumbs-up. He looked tired, worn out like dirty laundry.

I reached up and rang the bell, then took a step back with my clipboard tight against my chest. The door swung open. There was a lady standing there. She was wearing shiny black pants and a tight sweater zipped up to her jaw. She had a high, bouncy ponytail that twitched when she spoke.

"Hello," the lady said.

She nodded and smiled at me then stood on her tippy toes to look over my head at David. She waved. She didn't need to stand on her tippy toes to see but she did anyway.

"Are you selling cookie,s honey?"

"We sell treats."

"What's that?"

"Treats."

"Oh, perfect, I love treats."

Everything got tight, like my head was filling with air and my face got hot. That's how I felt sometimes when strangers looked at me. I'd get stuck if I had to do a presentation in front of the class, my tongue dry in my mouth, or my eyes would water when I had to lead a song in Clovers. The strange thing was, I wasn't afraid of the kids in class or the girls at Clovers. I just didn't like them looking at me.

"Don't be shy," the lady said. "You say your thing and I'll buy a box."

The lady nodded at the clipboard. I was gripping it so tight that the edges were pinching into my palms. I tried to read the pitch but the words blurred and jumped. I couldn't find where I was supposed to start.

"Um, we have Lays, Oreos—"

"So, you do have cookies."

"Yes."

"Perfect, I'll have one box, honey. Just one box."

I went down to the curb where David already had the box of Oreos ready.

"Way to go, he said."

I walked the Oreos back up to the lady. She handed me five dollars and I marked it down on the clipboard.

"You'll get better with practice."

"Thanks."

"Okay, have a good day."

The lady waved one last time at David and shut the door. At first, I couldn't move. My legs felt wobbly like I'd been running or swimming for a long time. I stepped away from the door and felt a lump, round like a pebble, rise at the back of my throat. Stupid, so stupid. And I'd have to do a hundred more. I got to the car and ducked down so my beret would hide my face, but David saw anyway.

"What's wrong?" he said. "Are you crying? Don't cry. Are you afraid? Hey, hey, it's okay. This is supposed to be fun."

I shook my head.

"I want Mom."

When I decided I wanted Joanne I felt it deep in my stomach. I was greedy with her, and I had a sense of this, that it wasn't something other children felt, but that knowledge only convinced me further that we were different, special. When I was little and had a nightmare, I always cried for Joanne. I hungered for my mother.

David drove right back to the house. He carried the boxes out of the car and stacked them in the garage.

"Don't worry. We can try again tomorrow. Practice makes perfect."

I pushed past him and the boxes, through the heavy garage door with the double lock, into the house. Joanne wouldn't pretend every hurt had a place. She knew about deep hurts, ones you couldn't kiss away. She let me be sad when she was sad. David was afraid of sad. He wanted everyone to be okay.

"Mommy," I called inside.

The house was silent. David came in from the garage after me.

"Joanne?"

There was no answer. He went to the bottom of the stairs and called up into the house.

"Joanne, we're home."

He started up the stairs.

"Let's find Mommy," he said.

Joanne was back in bed with all the covers pulled up over her. She was still, almost like a hill, a high ripple in a pale blue field. I leaned up against the foot of the bed and David sat down beside her.

Near her, I already felt better. Curled up on her side, my mother was like a sleeping mountain spirit, powerful and silent, storing up magic for later so she could be bold and make beautiful things in the studio. Landscapes and magnificent portraits that were as bright as photographs, but better than photographs because they were made, not taken. I wanted to crawl into bed and lean against the mountain. Rest my head against her back and listen for the deep rumble of her breath.

David reached deep into the sheets and scooped Joanne up by the armpits. It was like a trick, a naked rabbit pulled from a hat. There she was, the inside of the mountain scooped out, her arms soft and pink.

"No," Joanne moaned.

She slumped forward. Her hands were bent in her lap like two twigs snapped off a tree.

"Jo, you have to eat," David said. "Won't you eat something, today?"

Joanne whispered something I couldn't hear.

"That's okay," David said. "We love you."

Joanne kicked her legs out and they shot under the covers toward the end of the bed. I jumped back.

"Shh," David said, still holding her up under the armpits. "We can go to the hospital if you want. What do you think, Jo? Do you want to go to the hospital?"

"No," I said.

"Naomi." David's voice was like a warning.

"I don't want her to see me like this," Joanne said.

David glanced back at me.

"Just five minutes, okay?"

"No," I said. I wanted to scream. I needed my mother.

"Yes, just five minutes and then Mom will come down."

I shook my head and felt the pebble rise in my throat again. I was going to cry, but not because I was sad. I hated David. The hospital was for emergencies only. I tried to say that but instead my voice broke in a sob. I ran out of the room and down the stairs.

I sat on the last step and cried until my whole face was wet, right down to my chin. It felt good and vicious to get it out. When I was done, I sniffed hard and wiped my face with the back of my hand. Then I listened for their voices. David warbled above me like a tuba underwater. Joanne was silent.

At the bottom of the stairs, I had an idea. The kind of idea that flared up suddenly, like it had been whispered in your ear by the worst part of yourself. Kids have those ideas as much as grown-ups but are more likely to test them out, to see what happens. I got up and crept into the garage. I switched the light on and closed the door gently behind me. The boxes of treats were stacked where David left them.

I knelt down beside a box of Cracker Jacks and started to pick at one end of the box until the tape came up. There were red- and white-striped bags with a boy dressed as a sailor and a little dog on the label. There were at least 50 bags. I'd never sell them all. I reached into the box for a bag. I shook it and a few candies rattled around inside. It was mostly air.

I decided to get rid of the treats. Not all of them, but most. Then I wouldn't have to spend so much time selling them to strangers. I could spend more time at home with Joanne. I'd take care of her and they'd forget about the hospital.

I stood up and stuffed the bag up my T-shirt. I patted it and the bag crunched against my belly. I got four more bags and stuffed those up my shirt as well. I stuck the tape back down over the box and moved the stack around so the box of Cracker Jacks was at the bottom. Then I went back inside the house.

I paused at the stairs and waited for the creak of the floor overhead. Everything was quiet. David wasn't talking anymore. I held the Cracker Jacks in place under my shirt and went carefully through the kitchen and out the back door onto the deck.

Joanne's clogs were beside the door. I put them on. They were too big and with each step my feet slipped forward so my toes touched the end. I walked slowly. It was grey out and the cloudy sky was starting to fade. I made it to the end of the deck and cut across the yard to the back fence. There was a little hole where the wood had gone rotten. I squatted down and slipped through sideways. I just fit. Soon I'd be too big.

I knew not to go too far into the forest because I might fall into the ravine, so I walked forward just 20 steps, my feet slipping in the clogs the whole way. I found a good spot where the ground went soft and opened the bottom of my shirt, so the bags of Cracker Jacks tumbled out.

I found a stick and pushed it into the ground. It was soft. I got down on my knees and scooped the dirt away. I didn't mind getting dirty. Neither did Joanne. I arranged the Cracker Jacks in a hole and pushed the dirt back over top of them, covering all the sailor boys and their dogs. I arranged a few sticks and dead leaves over the top to disguise the hole and make it blend in. Then I stood up, rubbed my hands off down the front of my jeans, and studied my work.

The ground was smooth again. I imagined, because I'd put the Cracker Jacks in the ground with love, that they'd grow like seeds into trees. They'd grow little buds of candied popcorn, taste sweet and sappy. I kicked one more rock over the spot for good measure and then headed back for the house.

❖

That night, David fell asleep on the couch with the TV on, flickering blue across the family room. Joanne was up working in her studio. Sometimes when she stayed in bed all day, she got a bit better at night.

Joanne worked on the walls, painting blackbirds. They started small, growing out of a crack in the baseboard, and then grew, stretching across the walls with pointed wings and sharp talons. She worked around the easel and table for mixing paint, pulled the desk away from the wall and stood up on the cabinet for art supplies. I sat cross-legged in the middle of the studio and watched my mother spread black paint thick over the walls. Tubes of paint and brushes were scattered across the floor.

"I don't want to do Clovers," I said.

Joanne set her brush down and sat on the floor across from me.

"Maybe you can stay home with me instead."

"Okay."

Joanne reached for me and we rocked back and forth. I tilted my head back to look at the birds and Joanne shivered so I rubbed her back. The birds were a bit frightening. Joanne left blank spaces where their eyes should have been.

My mother sighed and tilted her head to rest on my shoulder.

"I'm afraid today," she whispered.

I felt something shift then, there in the studio, sitting under the birds. It was like Joanne needed me very much, greedy and stubborn, like she might lift my shirt up and rub her face against my belly.

"I'll keep you safe," I whispered back. When I did, I knew something had changed, but I didn't know it was forever. I meant what I said.

After that, I didn't have to do Clovers anymore. A little part of David gave up and I could tell that made him sad, but I didn't care. I never went back to check on my Cracker Jacks in the forest. I found, suddenly, that I was very busy. I worried about Joanne often. At school, I would watch the clock all afternoon, counting down the minutes until I could go home. I chewed my lips until they cracked and bled. David got me a special lip chap from the pharmacy that smelled like pine needles. I had to put it on five times a day.

The air got colder and months passed. The ground froze and it snowed early. David made everyone go outside into the backyard and we pushed together a snowman. We caught snowflakes on our tongues and Joanne laughed for the first time in a long time. She didn't feel like a ghost then, or a witch, or magic. She felt like a normal mother. I'd almost forgotten she could be like that.

With the trees bare, I could see back into the forest from the yard, right to the spot where I buried the Cracker Jacks. I could see it wasn't very far at all. I could remember the way I imagined the tree, with the little popped buds, but I couldn't see it in my mind in the same way, like a picture. Something was different and make-believing a Cracker Jack tree felt like a very stupid thing to do.

David painted over the blackbirds in the studio and Joanne didn't have to go to the hospital. We were happy together, but something was different. I felt it between Joanne and me, the way she clung to my sleeve when David wasn't looking and asked strange questions, like if I knew what would happen when we died or if Hell was real. Joanne was really afraid of these things. They kept her awake at night and I didn't have the right answers. The questions frightened me. They made me realize death for the first time, the painful truth of it, the great blackness at the end of all things.

And I realized that time was moving. I was getting older, and Joanne and David were too. I realized then, that Joanne would die one day and the stubborn, greedy love in my belly twisted and became desperate. I didn't want her to die.

Every night after David and Joanne kissed me goodnight, I'd stay up, and whisper into the dark, "*Please don't take my Mommy.*" It was a hopeless little thing to say. I couldn't become the child again or relearn how to make believe or find the right answers for Joanne. At night, I dreamed of blackbirds, their eyes empty holes, and when I woke up in the night, I didn't call out for my mother.

Thank you to Evan, Amanda, Albert, Theresa, and Chris.
Thank you to the Exile team, Michael, Barry,
Bruce, and Randall.

And I would like to gratefully acknowledge
that the book was written with support from
the Toronto Arts Council and the Ontario Arts Council.

Thank you to all my teachers.